To Clark
from
Jenny & Jim.

1945

DAVE DAWSON
WITH
THE R.A.F.

by

R. SIDNEY BOWEN

Author of
"DAVE DAWSON AT DUNKIRK"

*"Clark" from Jimmy
for a very Happy "Birthday"*

Sept-21-1945

THE SAALFIELD PUBLISHING COMPANY

AKRON, OHIO • NEW YORK

CONTENTS

		PAGE
I	TWO JUNKERS LESS!	9
II	MYSTERIOUS ORDERS	24
III	NIGHT RAID	34
IV	NAZI WINGS OVER LONDON	47
V	AIR VICE-MARSHAL SAUNDERS	68
VI	ENGLAND MUST NEVER DIE	84
VII	BRAVE WINGS FLY EASTWARD	101
VIII	TERROR RIDES THE NIGHT SKY	115
IX	IN THE ENEMY'S COUNTRY	128
X	TRAPPED!	141
XI	FLIGHT FROM NAZI GUNS	157
XII	QUICK THINKING	175
XIII	SIXTEEN RUE CHARTRES	194
XIV	PIERRE DESCHAUD SPEAKS	210
XV	DANGER IN THE DARK	223
XVI	WINGS OF THE R.A.F.	237

CHAPTER ONE

Two Junkers Less!

DAVE DAWSON lay on his back, fingers laced behind his head for a pillow, and lazily watched white patches of cloud play tag with each other at some eighteen thousand feet over England. It was the tenth day of September, 1940, and the most glorious summer the British had experienced in forty years was still very much in evidence. The sun was a brassy ball in the heavens that flooded the earth with a warm comforting glow. The birds, the bees, and the butterflies were all around. And the emerald green of the surrounding landscape gave him the feeling that the snow and the cold of winter were two things that would never be experienced in England again.

A perfect summer day! The warm sun, the singing birds, the flowers in bloom—and the war! Twenty miles across the English Channel, less than three minutes by air, Nazi hordes were working day and night toward that great moment when their leader, Adolf Hitler, would give them the order to begin their attempted invasion of England. And on this side of that Channel some forty odd millions of people were also working day and night so that when the order was given, not a single German booted foot would succeed in touching English soil. A beautiful summer day, and the people of the greatest empire on earth were waiting, ready to fight and die to the last man that their empire might continue to survive.

"Well, Pilot Officer Dave Dawson, of His Majesty's Royal Air Force," a voice suddenly spoke in Dave's ear, "I'll give you a penny for your thoughts. No, wait, let me guess. You were thinking about your home in Boston, Massachusetts, back in the States?"

Dave sat up and grinned down at the good-looking, sun-bronzed youth sprawled out on the grass at his side. He shook his head and held out his hand.

"Wrong, Pilot Officer Freddy Farmer, of the same Royal Air Force," he said. "So pay me the penny. I was thinking that it sure is one swell day. And I was wondering if we were going to get a little action, or if Hitler had found out we were now regular active service pilots, and had decided to call off the war."

"Hardly," the English youth said with a chuckle. "True, he's probably scared stiff now that you and I are in the R.A.F. I fancy, though, he isn't that scared. But it's pretty wonderul, isn't it? I mean, to be in the R.A.F."

Dave didn't answer. He let his gaze wander over to the line of Supermarine Spitfires powered with 1030 hp. Rolls Royce "Merlin" engines. Just looking at those swift, man-made metal birds of war made his heart start pounding and the blood surge through his body. An honest to goodness Spitfire pilot in the Royal Air Force! It was like living a wonderful dream, and it was doubly wonderful because it was true. The training and the concentrated study were all behind Freddy and himself, now. Each wore the highly prized wings above the

upper left pocket of his tunic. But perhaps even
more important was the fact that they had already received their baptism under fire. Each
had got himself a German plane, the first pay-
ment in return for the training and instruction
England had given them. For a month, now,
they had been stationed with No. 207 Squadron,
located on the east coast of England, just a few
miles north of Chelmsford. Only a month so
far on active duty—the "Babies" of the Squadron—but because of the speed with which wars
are being fought these days, with each day filled
with twenty-four hours of service and activity,
they were just as much veterans as most of the
older pilots.

"Stop daydreaming," Freddy cut into Dave's
thoughts. "You are glad to be in the R.A.F.,
aren't you?"

Dave looked at him and raised both his eyebrows.

"Glad?" he echoed. "Boy, I'm tickled pink!
Right now I wouldn't swap places with anybody else in all the world. Glad? Holy smokes!
Is that a dumb question! And say, come across
with that penny. Pay up, pal!"

Freddy made a face, fished a penny from his pocket and tossed it over.

"Right you are, there," he said. "I'll have you know an Englishman always pays his debts. What do you think, Dave?"

"About what?"

"About the blighters across the Channel," Freddy said. "Think they'll be fools enough to try and invade us? I mean, seriously."

"I don't know," Dave said with a shrug. He plucked a blade of grass and started chewing on it thoughtfully. "No, I don't know if Hitler's that crazy, or not," he continued after a moment. "All I can say is I sure hope he tries it. We'll give him a beating he won't forget in a hurry. Gee! That makes me feel good!"

"What makes you feel good?" Freddy wanted to know.

"Saying that," Dave grunted. "Saying *we'll* give him a beating. Gosh, a few months ago I was an American citizen, standing on the sidelines watching things. Now, though, I'm a part of it. When I speak of England doing this or that, I'm including me, because I'm really a little part of it, now. It sure gives me a kick to feel that way, and to know it's true."

"And England is grateful, Dave," Freddy said solemnly. "I guess you might say that England's fighting to save the world, and—"

The young Englishman didn't finish the rest. At that moment the phone bell in the Dispersal Office not far away rang harshly. In a flash they were both on their feet, because the ringing of that phone bell always meant just one thing. It meant that German planes had been sighted approaching 207's patrol area. The voice at the other end of that phone would state where the planes were, how many in number, the types, the altitude, direction, and so forth. To pilots on stand-to duty the ringing of that bell meant action coming up. And so, as their flight leader answered the call, Dave and Freddy started pulling on their helmets and zipping up their flying suits, for although it was summer on the ground it was cold up around twenty thousand feet where they usually did battle.

A moment later Flight Lieutenant Barton-Woods, leader of their flight, known as Green Flight, came dashing out of the Dispersal Office.

"Right-o, chaps!" he called out to them, and hurried toward his plane. "A couple of Junkers

88s cutting across Zone H at twenty-two thousand. Let's go up and chase the beggars down into the sea."

In less than a minute the three Spitfires streaked off the field and went wind screaming up for altitude. As soon as they were clear, Flight Lieutenant Barton-Woods checked his radio with the field's station, and then checked with the two members of his flight.

"Radio check, chaps!" came the words in Dave's helmet phones.

"Check, sir," he spoke into the disc-shaped mike in front of his mouth.

"Check, also, sir," he heard Freddy sing out.

"Right you are, lads," the flight lieutenant replied. "Don't forget to turn on your oxygen at five thousand, so's you won't forget it at twenty."

Dave reached forward and turned the little valve knob that would feed him oxygen through a mouthpiece. He didn't need it yet, of course, but it was a practice to turn the thing on at low altitudes so that it would be ready for instant use at higher altitudes. If you waited until you needed oxygen, you might be too busy at that moment fighting for your life to have time to

turn the knob. And then it would be just too bad
—for you.

And so Dave made sure ahead of time, then
concentrated on keeping his place in the V-
shaped formation, and following his flight
leader high up into the cloud-dotted blue. In
less time than it takes to tell about it, England
was just a blur of browns and greens far down
under their wings; just a tiny island completely
surrounded by water and almost within broad
jumping distance of Nazi-conquered Europe.
Dave, however, didn't bother about admiring
the sight. He had seen it countless times before.
And besides, he needed his eyes now for things
above, not under him. Somewhere up in that
vast expanse of white-dotted blue two German
Junkers were trying to sneak in to drop their
bomb loads on English soil. Two of Air Mar-
shal Goering's winged vultures were hoping
to—

"There they are, chaps!" Flight Lieutenant
Barton-Woods' voice came through the earphones. "Turn right a quarter, and a thousand
feet above us. Tally-ho, lads! The blighters!
They spotted us and are turning back! After
them, Green Flight!"

Dave and Freddy had already spotted the two would-be raiders off to their right front and a thousand feet or so higher. The huge twin-engine craft were halfway around in a bank back toward the east, and the rays of the sun on their metal wings and sides made them look like prehistoric birds of glistening silver cutting through the air.

Keeping his eyes glued to them, Dave hunched forward slightly in his seat and slid one thumb up to rest on the trigger button on his control stick. One jab at that button and the eight Vickers high speed machine guns cowled into the Spitfire's wings, four on each side, would spew out a shower of destruction at the rate of over nine thousand bullets a minute. All eight guns were sighted to converge at a point some two hundred yards in front of the ship. And anything that crossed that spot when those eight guns were hammering out their song was doomed to a lot of trouble—and nine times out of ten just plain, naturally doomed.

For a split second Dave took his eyes off the Junkers trying to scoot back home and shot a quick glance at Freddy Farmer. His lips twisted back in a happy smile, and a warm comforting glow drifted through him. Good old Freddy. Always there just off his wingtip. A pilot in a million, as far as Dave was concerned. They flew like a team that had been working together for years instead of only a few months. Each seemed to sense instantly, whether on a routine practice patrol or in the middle of a bullet-barking dog fight, just what the other was going to do. And as a result of the perfect coordination between them, more times than not they got exactly what they went after. As Squadron Leader Trenton, 207's commanding officer, had once remarked:

"They're the babies of the Squadron, but I jolly well wish I had a whole squadron of babies!"

At that moment a short, savage burst from Flight Lieutenant Barton-Woods' guns snapped Dave's eyes back to the Junkers. They were still quite a ways off but the Green Flight leader had let go with a challenging burst hoping that the Germans would give up thoughts of escape and turn back to give battle. However, it was instantly obvious that the Junkers pilots and their crews didn't want any truck with three Spitfire pilots. The nose of each ship was pushed down a bit to add speed to the get away attempt. And a moment later Dave saw the flash of sunlight on bombs dropping harmlessly down into the rolling grey-green swells where the Channel blends in with the North Sea.

"Not this day, my little Jerries!" Flight Lieutenant Barton-Woods' voice boomed over the radio. "Let's make the beggars pay for dropping bombs in our Channel, Green Flight! Give it to them!"

The last was more or less the signal that each pilot was on his own. Dave waited until he saw his flight leader swerve off to slam in at the Junkers to the right. Then he touched rudder, and with Freddy sticking right with him, swerved off after the other German raider. They were real close now, well within gun range, and as the pair slid out to take up attack positions the Junkers' gunners started throwing nickel jacketed lead. The wavy smoke of tracers whipped and zipped by a few feet over Dave's head. He laughed into his mike and dropped his nose and cut sharply off to the right. Freddy did the same, only off to the left.

No sooner had they started the cutting away maneuver than they cut right back in again. The

German gunners saw them coming and fired their guns savagely, but those two R.A.F. lads tore in like a couple of man-made birds gone completely crazy. It was as though they both intended to fly right straight into the Junkers. Then when there were no less than a couple of split seconds left before just that would happen, Freddy Farmer's voice sang out in Dave's earphones.

"Right-o, Dave!" he shouted. "This one for us!"

They both jabbed their trigger button and sixteen Vickers machine guns poured a withering blast of destruction into that Junkers 88. For a few seconds the German raider continued to roar eastward. Then suddenly its port engine belched out a cloud of red flame and oily black smoke. Then as though the craft had hooked its left wing on some invisible wall in the sky, the Junkers staggered to the left and down. Its tail gunner kept up his fire as Dave and Freddy skipped past and zoomed up to dive attack again. But that German might just as well have tried to shoot at a couple of lightning bolts flashing by.

Cutting short their zoom Dave and Freddy rolled their Spitfires over and let them drop by the nose. Down they came again, holding their fire until the last few seconds. The Junkers now was more like a moving cloud of smoke than an airplane flying through the air. And when Dave and Freddy jabbed their trigger buttons again it was the death blow for that German raider. The right wing broke off clean at the stub, and carried the starboard engine along with it. From nose to tail the Junkers became no more than a moving ball of fire. Then suddenly the gas tanks let go. The whole sky was filled with barbs of darting flame and billowing clouds of black smoke. The sky trembled and shook . . . and then the Junkers 88 just wasn't there any more. It was a shower of smoking and flaming debris slithering down into the North Sea.

"Good lad, Dave!" Freddy sang out. "Your bursts did it!"

"My bursts, nothing!" Dave called back to him. "I didn't even come close to the guy. That was your plane, Freddy. Congratulations!"

"Rot!" Freddy snorted into his disc mike, also known as the "flap" mike. "We'll split the beggar and each take half, eh? Oh, oh, Dave! The flight lieutenant's in trouble!"

It was true. Perhaps there was a better pilot in the other Junkers, or perhaps gunners with a better aim, or it was even possible Flight Lieutenant Barton-Woods had become careless for a moment or so. Anyway, he had not nailed his man, and the Junkers gunners were giving him quite an uncomfortable time as he zoomed up into the clear. Dave and Freddy didn't speak a single word between them. They simply wheeled across the sky in perfect attack formation, and then roared down on the Junkers.

Its rear gunner was no novice, and he had courage. He stuck to his guns and returned their own savage fire. Dave felt his plane quiver slightly, and knew that German bullets were hitting his ship. But he didn't swerve an inch. His wing howled down at the German and he held his fire until the right moment. This time he shouted the signal.

"Smack it, Freddy!"

Their guns hammered and yammered out their song, and Dave could clearly see their tracers zinging down into the German plane. No man-made airplane on earth could have withstood that blasting fire from the sixteen guns between the two youths. And that Junkers 88 was no exception to prove the rule. It burst into flame and went careening crazily off on one wing. Then it dropped by the nose and started howling seaward in a vertical power dive. After it had dropped three or four hundred feet, five black dots popped out from it like peas out of a pod. They instantly became men in Dave's vision, and they slowly turned over and over as they fell down through the air. At the end of almost thirty seconds a puff of white shot up from each man's back. They spread out into parachute envelopes, and five German airmen drifted slowly down toward the surface of the North Sea where British motorboats waited to pull them in as captured prisoners.

Dave and Freddy didn't bother watching the five German airmen float downward. Instead they pulled up out of the dives, closed in on Flight Lieutenant Barton-Woods and took up formation positions. Their leader grinned at them, and they heard his voice coming over the radio.

"Stout work, you two," he said. "Made an awful mess of it, myself. But you two were along, so I knew everything would be fine. Well, let's toot on back home and report to the O.C."

CHAPTER TWO

Mysterious Orders

LESS THAN half an hour later, the three pilots of 207 were reporting all details of the patrol to Squadron Leader Trenton, and the R.A.F. Intelligence officer who sat at his side. No matter how trivial a patrol may be, R.A.F. pilots always make a complete report upon their return to the home field. That way the ranking powers are always able to have a complete picture of the war in the air before them. In other words, every single scrap of information about a patrol is important, because you never can tell what it might mean in the whole scheme of things. For that reason the pilots not only made out their reports in writing, but made them by word of mouth, too.

"Good work, you two," the Squadron Leader said, and smiled at Freddy and Dave. "It's not such an easy job getting a Junkers 88. Those planes have a pretty fair amount of fire power. So getting *two* of them is a mighty good piece of work. And, oh yes, stay a bit, will you? I want to have a talk with you."

A few minutes later Flight Lieutenant Barton-Woods and the Intelligence officer headed off for the mess. As the door closed on them, Squadron Leader Trenton swung around in his chair and gave the two boys a long piercing stare. Then he suddenly clasped his hands on the desk and leaned forward.

"I say, you two," he spoke up, "have you gotten yourselves into a bit of trouble that might have been reported to the Air Ministry in London?"

Dave and Freddy looked blankly at each other for a brief moment, then returned their gaze to the squadron leader.

"Trouble, sir?" Dave echoed faintly.

"When, sir?" Freddy added. "And where?"

The squadron commander shrugged and looked completely at sea.

"I haven't the faintest idea," he said. "I was only asking you. Nothing happened when you two popped up to London for a day's leave last week?"

"Why, no, sir," Freddy answered promptly for them both. "We just nosed around and saw a couple of shows, that's all. We were both back here at the squadron by midnight."

"Why?" Dave put the question. "Has anything happened, sir?"

"I can't say," Squadron Leader Trenton murmured, and stared at them with a troubled look in his eyes. "Just after you took off on this last show, I received a phone call from Air Ministry. You two are ordered to report to Air Vice-Marshal Saunders bright and early tomorrow morning. You'd better go up to London tonight so's you'll be sure and be at Adastral House (R.A.F. name for the Air Ministry) bright and early."

"Air Vice-Marshal Saunders?" Freddy Farmer repeated in an awed tone. "But why would he want to see us, sir?"

Squadron Leader Trenton smiled thinly as he gestured with his two hands on the desk.

"In this case, I still haven't any idea," he said. "Usually, though, it's for one of two reasons: to give you a very hot going over for breaking some rule and getting into trouble; or else to give you his personal congratulations as he tells you you've been recommended for a medal."

"Well, it surely can't be for either of those reasons," Dave said with a frown. "We certainly haven't bumped into any trouble, and we certainly haven't done anything to rate a medal. And— My gosh! Holy smokes! Do you suppose—?"

Dave gulped and didn't finish the rest. Squadron Leader Trenton gave him a keen glance.

"Do I suppose what, Dawson?" he prompted.

Dave had to swallow again before he could speak. A crazy thought had suddenly flashed through his brain, but just the same it had given him a cold chill.

"Do you suppose there's some new law?" he began. "I mean, could there be some new ruling that might force us to resign our commissions because we're both only seventeen, a year under the regulation age?"

A look of relief flooded the senior officer's face. He laughed and shook his head.

"Not even likely!" he said in firm conviction. "After the way you two chaps have stood up, it doesn't matter in the slightest how old you are— seventeen or seventy. No, Dawson, I think I can assure you positively that the R.A.F. will never make any new ruling or law that would rid it of you two. No, you can let that worry bail out of your mind, and forget it forever. No, that wasn't the reason for my phone call."

"And you really haven't *any* idea, sir?" Freddy asked. "I mean, could this possibly mean that Dawson and I are being transferred someplace else?"

"By gad, I hope not!" the squadron leader exclaimed sharply, and sat up in his chair. "No, it couldn't be that, either. I would be informed. The transfer papers would be sent along to me. Besides, I'd raise the roof at any suggestion like that."

"Boy, I wish we were reporting today," Dave grunted. "I know doggone well I won't sleep a wink tonight!"

"Which may be the exact truth!" Squadron Leader Trenton said with a dry smile. "The

Jerries are starting to bomb London at night, now, you know. And by the way, if they do while you two are there, just see to it that you keep out from under, won't you? It cost the R.A.F. a fair penny to make Spitfire pilots out of you. We want a return on the investment, you know."

The two boys laughed, but inside they glowed and felt very happy indeed. That was simply Squadron Leader Trenton's way of saying that he valued their aid to 207, and didn't want anything to happen that would rob 207 Squadron of their flying and combat ability.

"Don't worry, we'll sure watch our step, sir," Dave said. Then, with a quick side glance at Freddy: "I'll see that he doesn't stumble over any bombs. I'll keep hold of his hand all the time."

The squadron leader laughed, and Freddy Farmer blushed to the ears.

"When anybody has to hold my hand, I'll jolly well let you know!" the young Englishman said scornfully. "Like as not, it'll be the other way 'round. Don't you think his face is getting a bit pale already, sir?"

Freddy addressed the last to Squadron Leader Trenton, who laughed again.

"Can't say for sure, Farmer," the O.C. said gravely. "The light's bad in here, you know. Well, anyway, pop along, you two, and pack a bag. The adjutant will give you railroad vouchers, and your passes. Get back here soon. And no matter what—good luck to both of you."

The two youths thanked him, saluted and retreated outside. As they started toward their living quarters, Dave slyly stuck out his foot, and when Freddy tripped over it and started to fall headlong, Dave grabbed him quickly.

"See?" Dave chided, as he helped Freddy to keep his balance. "Just as I thought! You need somebody to hold your hand. Oh, well, I'll be glad to do it, because I like you, little boy. *Hey!*"

Freddy caused the exclamation, because as he straightened up he stepped hard on Dave's foot, then broke into a sprint for their living quarters. The English youth won by a good three yards. He was inside and hauling out his suitcase as Dave came bursting in. He glanced up with a look of mock concern on his face.

"Something wrong, Dave?" he murmured. "Is a Jerry chasing you?"

"Just a pal!" Dave growled, and limped toward his own bunk. "I stop the guy from falling down and breaking his neck, and what does he do? He practically cripples me for life. A fine screw-ball I've got for a pal. Say, Freddy?"

"Yes?"

Dave sank down on his bunk with a frown and made no effort to haul out his suitcase.

"This business at Adastral House tomorrow," he grunted. "Jeepers! I sure hope it isn't bad news. I don't know why, but I've got a funny feeling."

Freddy stopped packing and looked up.

"What kind of a funny feeling?" he wanted to know.

Dave scratched the back of his neck and sighed.

"Just a funny feeling, that's all," he said. "I can't put it into words. I've just got a hunch that plenty is going to happen."

"Good, or bad?" Freddy asked.

Dave shook his head and got off the bunk.

"Boy, do I wish I knew!" he breathed. "Well, we can only wait and hope, I guess. Where do you want to stay in London? Your family's house on Baker Street is closed up, isn't it?"

"Yes," Freddy said. "But, if you like, we can open it for the night. There'd be no objections."

"No, let's bunk at a hotel," Dave said. "How about the Savoy? That's close to the Air Ministry."

"So the lad's a blinking millionaire!" Freddy commented with a chuckle. "He must stay at the very best of places. Too bad they don't rent room and bath at Buckingham Palace."

"Okay, okay!" Dave growled. "Then where do we park?"

"Why, at the Savoy, of course," Freddy said with a sly grin. "I fancy our pilot officer's pay can stand it for one night. And that makes me wonder a bit, you know?"

"What does?" Dave asked absently, as he started studying a London timetable. "What are you wondering about now, my little man?"

"I was wondering where we'll be *tomorrow* night," Freddy replied.

"Somehow I don't even dare guess," Dave said. "And—Hey, get a move on, fellow! There's a train leaving Chelmsford in forty minutes. Let's grab that. It gets us in London just about in time to put on the feed bag. Gee! I wonder if they've got strawberry shortcake at the

Savoy. Boy, can I go for that dish!"

"Good grief!" Freddy groaned. Then, in mock gravity: "Why, certainly, my dear fellow. Anything for a weary R.A.F. pilot, you know. After all, who else is fighting the blinking war?"

Dave heaved a book at him, but Freddy dodged it neatly, and then the pair set to packing in earnest. As they expected to be away only a day and a night at the most, they didn't put many "spares" into their bags. As a matter of fact, though, had the two of them been able to look into the future at that moment, they wouldn't have bothered about packing anything! Clean shirts, spare socks and handkerchiefs, and all that sort of stuff, were items they wouldn't be even thinking about in the hectic days that lay just ahead.

"Okay, I'm set, are you?" Dave presently announced, and clicked his bag shut.

"Right you are," Freddy called out, and shut his own bag. "Off we go!"

Dave caught up his bag and started for the door. When he reached it, he suddenly paused and turned around.

"Doggone that hunch!" he grunted. "Wonder what it means, anyway?"

CHAPTER THREE

Night Raid

THE SHRILL whistle of the locomotive echoed across the twilight-steeped English countryside. The train lurched and trembled for a moment or so, and then started gliding smoothly along the tracks. Dave and Freddy took a last glance out the compartment window at the Chelmsford station and then settled back comfortably on the cushioned seats. They had the compartment to themselves, and for that they were truly grateful. They were headed for London for half leave and half military reasons, but that didn't mean they weren't tired. The last few weeks had been crowded with more aerial warfare than had taken place in a whole year in World War

34

Number One. The Royal Air Force had almost single-handed held back the Nazis from crossing the Channel. Still outnumbered, but not so much as at Dunkirk, the R.A.F. boys from the squadron leaders right down to the lowest grade mechanics had gained mastery of the air over the Channel and over England. And, what was more important, they had held that mastery regardless of the German fleets of planes Goering had hurled against them.

Stretching out, Dave leaned his head back, and cocked his feet up on the opposite seat.

"If I could only get Air Vice-Marshal Saunders off my mind," he sighed, "I might catch me a bit of shut-eye. Boy, we've been hitting that old ball lately, you know?"

"Hitting what?" Freddy murmured, and closed his eyes. "What in the world does that mean?"

"Sure, hitting the old ball," Dave said lazily. "Smacking that apple. Hitting on all six. Right on the beam every minute. Catch on?"

"Oh, of course!" Freddy groaned, and gave a shake of his head. "A chap who spoke English would certainly be at a loss in the States, wouldn't he?"

"That's right," Dave said sleepily. "Just like an American being in England. Lift, for elevator! Treacle, when it's syrup! Queue-up, when you mean standing in line. Boy, what a language! And, am I all in! Jeepers! Am I tired! Am I—"

The sudden and abrupt slackening of the train's speed woke both boys up in a flash. In fact, it woke them up in the dark, for it was late evening outside, and while they had dozed the conductor had come in and pulled down the compartment window curtains. A very pale blue light in the corridor outside was of no more good than no light at all.

Freddy groaned aloud, flexed his stiff muscles, and peered around a corner of the window curtain.

"Now what?" he murmured. "Dark as pitch outside, but I'm sure we're not even close to London yet. I say, hear those anti-aircraft guns?"

"With both ears," Dave said, and took a squint out himself.

By pressing close to the glass and trying to look in the direction of the engine, he could just barely see the long pencil-thin beams of searchlights raking the heavens far ahead. And every now and then the dark sky was stabbed by blotches of flaming red and crimson.

"The Jerries are over again, trying to hit some more women and children," he said grimly. "I hope our night boys get every darn one of them."

"They'll get some, I fancy," Freddy said quietly. "But why are we running so slow? That raid is miles and miles ahead of us. Besides, I always thought a moving target was much harder to hit. This blasted train might just as well go sixty miles as six, as it must be doing now."

"Stay after school, Pilot Officer Farmer!" Dave snorted. "And here I thought you knew all the answers! My, my!"

"Oh, come off it!" Freddy snapped. "I suppose you know the reason?"

"Sure," Dave said.

"Well, what is it?"

"An official secret," Dave said in a hoarse whisper. "I'd tell you, but how do I know there isn't a Nazi agent under the seat?"

"*You'll* be under the seat, if you don't cut it out!" Freddy whispered back at him. "Now, what's the great reason?"

"Okay, if you've got to know," Dave said in a patient, resigned voice. "This is how it is, my little man. German planes carry bombs, and when they get over here they drop those bombs, see? Well, one might drop on the track way ahead of a train going sixty miles an hour, see? Well, maybe the engineer couldn't stop in time, and the train would pile up. But if the train crawls along until the all-clear is sounded, then the engineer can stop it on a dime if he should go around a curve and suddenly see a nice big bomb crater where the tracks should be. Now, right or wrong?"

Freddy made clucking sounds with his tongue in the darkness.

"Why, I believe the chap is right," he said, as though talking to himself. "Yes, I fancy he has a little bit of something useful between those big ears of his. You are right, of course, Dave."

"Ever see me when I was wrong?" Dave taunted. Then quickly: "No, let's not bring that up! Hey! Those planes are headed this way!"

Dave could have saved his breath on the last. As though a huge invisible door in the sky had been opened, the thunder of the guns tripled in sound. The compartment was suddenly bathed in the pale reflection of a battery of searchlight beams that suddenly sprang into action less than fifty yards from the tracks. The train had come to a full halt now, with its headlight turned off. A moment later came the familiar drone of night-bombing Heinkels and Benz-Daimler powered Focke-Wulf 187s above the roar of the batteries of anti-aircraft guns.

For a moment Dave and Freddy watched the approach of the raiding planes. Then common sense got the best of curiosity. They stretched out on the compartment floor beside each other to protect themselves as much as possible in case any of those eggs of death should happen to land near the train. Perhaps they looked funny huddling down on the compartment floor in their best Sunday-go-to-meeting uniforms. However, in England it is not a sign of being afraid or of cowardice to fling yourself flat when the bombers come over. It is a sign of good sense. Perhaps it is true that the bomb or bullet that gets you has your name on it, and you can't escape it no matter where you are. At the same time, though, only a fool or a madman deliberately dares a bomb to do him harm.

And so Freddy and Dave hugged the floor

while the raiders roared over and plastered the countryside with their loads of death and destruction. At least fifty times an earth-shaking roar, and a towering sheet of flame, made them think that was the last bomb they'd ever hear in this war, or in this world. Each time invisible hands seemed to reach down out of that roaring, flame-filled night sky and lift the train clear up off the tracks, and then let it drop back with a jarring crash. After each outburst, however, they continued to remain alive. And presently the throbbing drone died away in the distance, the roaring and barking of the guns ceased, and the searchlight beams winked out one by one. Night returned again to that section of England—night painted here and there with the glow of fires set by the bombs.

"The big bums!" Dave growled, and got up off the floor. "As if you and I haven't got enough to worry about without them buzzing over to make things worse. Were you scared, Freddy?"

"Stiff," the English youth promptly replied.

"Me, too," Dave said with half a chuckle. "That's my knees you hear, still knocking together. And they say you get used to air raids. Oh boy!"

"You probably do," Freddy said. "But I have no desire to prove it to myself. I hope the blighters didn't hit the track. It's a long walk from here to London. I say, what's that?"

At that moment a burst of shots had shattered the comparative silence outside. Regardless of regulations, the boys threw up their compartment window and leaned out. They saw a figure stumbling through the shadows alongside the train. He was bent over double as though in pain, and his footsteps faltered. Just as he came abreast of their compartment some more shots rang out. The stumbling figure stumbled for the last time. He fell forward, flat on his face, and lay still. In a few seconds half a dozen men in uniform came rushing up. One of them flashed a light on the still figure, then bent down and rolled him over.

"Well, that's one blighter they won't be able to count on from now on!" a voice growled. "A jolly good thing he's finished, too!"

"Right!" a second voice said. "If we hadn't been a patrol, it might have turned out a mess for this train. Fancy the beggar trying to let them know where it was!"

"I say there!" Freddy called, and leaned farther out the window. "What's all this?"

"Keep back in that train, and—!" a voice started to say, but stopped as the flashlight beam caught Dave and Freddy for a second in its glow. "Oh, sorry, sir," the same voice spoke again. "Thought you were just nosy civilians, not R.A.F. Well, sir, we caught another one of them Fifth Column beggars trying to do us harm."

"Yes, sir; that's right, sir," another voice broke in. "We were on our usual patrol along the track when suddenly we saw some bloke slinking along ahead of us. The raiders weren't even close, then, so we just followed this beggar and didn't challenge him. Well, strike me pink, sir, if he didn't drop down on the tracks, and whip one of them red flare things from his pocket and start to light it."

"But he didn't get away with it, I can tell you, sir," the first voice spoke up. "Me and Harry, here, right ups and jumps on him before he's even got the match to it. But he's a strong one, and he gives us a bit of a fight, and—"

"A bit of a fight?" the other voice interrupted again. "The blighter tosses us around like we're a couple of rag dolls, and starts scooting down the track. By then the bombers are right over us, and— Well, I guess you heard the things they dropped. Anyway, we lose this blighter for a bit during the mess-up. Then we spot him trying to get on the train. We don't bother to challenge, now. We just let him have what he deserves. And here he is. A good thing, too!"

"A *very* good thing," Freddy added. "Congratulations. You're air raid wardens, aren't you?"

"That's right, sir," one of them replied. "Too old for any regular military work, but we're jolly well glad to do what we can to help."

Dave looked down at the still figure on the ground. But for the watchfulness and constant vigilance of those "old" men, that dead Nazi spy might have lighted the signal flare on the track and made it possible for the German bombers overhead to see the slow moving train. But for those "old" men a bomb might have come screaming down to strike the train and blow one Dave Dawson and one Freddy Farmer straight into the next world. Dave glanced up at the men, and his eyes glowed with frank and open admiration.

"And without your help," he said, "England would be in a pretty tough spot. She can thank you fellows for a lot—and how!"

The air raid wardens chuckled in an embarrassed sort of way.

"Well, thank you, sir," one of them said. "It's mighty nice of you to put it that way. We're glad to do our bit, though. You sound like a Yank, sir."

"Oh, don't mind that," Freddy spoke up with a laugh before Dave could say a word. "You'd be surprised how he mangled the language at first. But he's really doing awfully well—for a little fellow. The squadron commander's going to let him taste his first cup of tea next week. And— *Ouch!*"

Dave had eased off the window catch so that it slid down on Freddy's neck. He held it there with his hands and grinned at the air raid wardens through the glass. They roared with laughter. Then as the train started to move, Dave released Freddy's neck and pushed the window up.

"Good luck!" he shouted, and leaned out. "Thumbs up, mates!"

"The same to you, sir!" they shouted back. "Thumbs up, R.A.F.!"

The train picked up speed, and another little incident in the war careers of Dave Dawson and Freddy Farmer became history. They closed the window, pulled the curtain down, and sank back on the seats. Freddy rubbed the back of his neck and glared at Dave's grinning face.

"Go ahead and grin, you queer-looking ape," he muttered. "But I'll get back at you, no fear. And when I do, you'll jolly well know it, too."

"Let that be a lesson to you to speak of your superiors in the future with more respect," Dave chuckled. "You're lucky, my little man, I didn't make you keep your head hanging out there all the way to London. But, gee, you English are certainly swell people!"

"Naturally," Freddy said in mock gravity. "Look who we are, my dear fellow. And just think how fortunate you are to have the opportunity to observe and learn."

"No kidding, though," Dave said, "Hitler's just hasn't a chance. It gave me a great kick to meet those air raid wardens back there."

"I know what you mean," Freddy said, and nodded. "It isn't just the Army, and the Navy, and the Air Force fighting Hitler, now. It's England—all of England from the oldest right down to the youngest."

"What a dope Hitler was even to think he could get away with it!" Dave murmured. "Boy, oh boy! Is that guy riding for one big fall!"

"And I jolly well hope it will be soon!" Freddy echoed. "And that reminds me. I certainly wish I knew what Air Vice-Marshal Saunders wants of us!"

Dave groaned and slid down on the seat.

"My pal!" he sighed unhappily. "Just when I was all nice and relaxed, you'd have to go and bring *that* up!"

CHAPTER FOUR

Nazi Wings Over London

DAVE GAVE the bell-hop a shilling and waited for the boy to step out into the hall and close the door. Then he took three running steps, jumped, and landed flat on his back on the bed. The springs squeaked in protest but didn't give way. Dave flung out his arms and sighed loudly.

"Boy, a real bed!" he exclaimed. "Look, Freddy, this is a bed. Springs, mattress, sheets, blankets, and everything. And it's all mine until tomorrow. Of course those things we have out at the squadron aren't too tough. But this! This is a real bed. Turn out that light, pal. I'm practically asleep right now. Gosh! That train took a million years, didn't it?"

Freddy didn't reply at once. He slung his suit-case onto the other bed, then came over and grabbed Dave by the feet. A good yank and Dave was on the floor.

"You're not using that bed, yet," Freddy grinned down into his startled face. "There's plenty of time for your beauty sleep. First we're going out to have a look at the black-out."

"Going out?" Dave groaned and got slowly to his feet. "Me go out and crack my shins against things in the dark? Nit, nat, no, my little man. Mrs. Dawson's pride and joy is going to bed. And I'm not kidding."

Freddy grinned wickedly and dropped into a wrestler's crouch.

"You think so?" he murmured. "Right you are! Just try and get into that bed."

"So that's it, huh?" Dave grunted and took a cautious step forward. "I've got to tie and gag you first? Or maybe you didn't hear me. *I'm* going to bed. You take London and the black-out. Me, I'm taking the bed. I—"

Dave cut the last off short and leaped for-ward, but Freddy was too quick for him. The English youth darted to the side, then turned in a flash and caught Dave's arms and pinned them behind his back.

"Do you go quietly with me, my little American chap?" he said. "Or shall I phone down for the Savoy Hotel manager to come up here and give me a hand?"

Dave struggled for a second or two, but was unable to break his friend's hold.

"Darned if the youngster hasn't a little bit of strength, at that!" he said in mocking surprise. "I'd better not be so easy with him after this. Okay, you win. Stop breaking my arms."

"We go for a walk?" Freddy asked, still keeping his hold.

"Okay, we walk," Dave said, and groaned wearily. "But if you fall down a man-hole—and you know what I hope—don't go yelling at me for help."

Freddy released his grip and stepped quickly backward. Dave rubbed his arms and scowled at him.

"Yeah, you do know a couple of tricks, don't you," he grunted. "But look. Why can't we see London in the daytime, when it's light? I'm dead on my feet, no kidding. You'd—"

Dave didn't finish. At that moment the familiar but always nerve-rasping wail of the air raid siren filled the night air outside. Freddy jumped across the room, and flipped off the light switch. Then the two went over to the window and pulled aside the black-out curtains. Far to the east the black sky was being stabbed by long pencils of white light that slowly swung back and forth from horizon to horizon. In a moment there came the dull pounding of distant anti-aircraft batteries. The sound grew louder and sharper as it drew near. Suddenly both boys jumped as a- battery nearby went into savage, furious action. It was so close it seemed practically under their feet.

"Holy smokes!" Dave gulped, and backed away from the window. "I swear I saw those shells going right up past the end of my nose. Get back from that window, Freddy. Concussion might blow in that glass and do plenty to your face. Let's—"

Br-r-rump!

The sound of an exploding bomb a few blocks away cut Dave's words off short. He looked at Freddy, and they both grinned sheepishly.

"I guess you're right!" Dave exclaimed. "I'm not going to bed. Let's go borrow a couple of tin helmets from the manager, if he has any, and go up on the roof."

"The roof?" Freddy echoed, and his eyes widened suddenly. "What in the world?"

Wha-a-ang! Br-r-rump!

Two bombs let go in rapid succession. They seemed to explode almost right outside the window. Dave and Freddy threw themselves flat on the floor between the twin beds, and held their breath. The hotel rocked and shook violently, and there was the tinkle of glass as the shattered window spilled into the room. They waited until the echo of the explosions had died away, and then got slowly to their feet. There was just a hole now where the window had been —a hole that looked out on a world gone suddenly mad with roaring sound and flashing red, orange and yellow flame. Freddy groped for Dave's hand and shook it warmly.

"Thanks, very much," he said in a tight voice.

"Thanks?" Dave murmured. "For what?"

"For reminding me to keep away from windows during a bombing raid," Freddy said. "But just before that blighter scared ten years off my life, what were you saying? Oh, yes. You want to go up on the roof?"

"Sure," Dave said with a nod. "For a look. We'll be as safe there as any place. If one's coming, it'll come. Just standing here waiting gives me the creeps, anyway."

"Me, too," Freddy agreed. "Let's go, then. Bet the manager's in the raid shelter, though, and won't dig up tin helmets for us for love nor money."

"Well, we can try," Dave said. "And— Drop, Freddy! Here comes another!"

Dave's words of warning were just a waste of breath. The screaming whistle of that bomb hurtling downward cut through all sound. As Dave flung himself flat again, he had the crazy feeling of listening to some huge invisible giant tearing off the top of the world. Even the anti-aircraft battery close to the hotel was drowned out by the unearthly sound of that falling bomb. Then it struck, and the hotel seemed to rise right straight up in the air. Dave was sure he could feel the floor heave under him. He closed his eyes tight, and held his breath. For a long moment everything seemed to stop dead. Then the hotel settled back like something alive but so very, very tired. A second later there was a short series of sharp cracking sounds, and ceiling plaster fell down on the two R.A.F. pilots.

"That baby was trying to mean business!" Dave said, and got to his feet again. "Hitler must know we're in town, the way so many of them are coming close. Hey, that *did* hit close. The building next door!"

The hole where the window had been was now like the entrance to a long blazing tunnel. Thirty feet away the three upper floors of a building were blazing fiercely. And when the two boys leaped over to the window hole, they saw that the entire front of the building had been torn away by the terrific blast. In the glow of the flames they could see right into rooms full of broken and mangled furniture and apartment furnishings. On the rear wall of one room was a framed picture of King George and Queen Elizabeth. Everything else in the room was wrecked beyond possible recognition by its owners, but the picture of the King and Queen was untouched. It hung on the blast-scorched wall as straight as could be.

Something about that picture hanging there touched a note deep in Dave Dawson. He stared at it for a moment in almost reverent awe. Then, clicking his heels, he brought his hand up in smart salute.

"There'll always be an England," he murmured softly.

Freddy Farmer caught the direction of his gaze, looked himself and saluted in turn.

"Always!" he said with deep tenderness in his voice.

At that moment a shrill cry of pain came to them from out of the burning building. There was a second cry, and a third. They could see nothing but the fierce glow of the flames, but the cries seemed to come from the rear of the fourth floor.

"There are wounded people in that building!" Freddy cried.

"Trapped, and probably can't get out!" Dave added. "And it's a cinch their cries can't be heard by the fire wardens down there in the street. What say, Freddy?"

"Of course!" the English youth shouted, and went bounding for the door.

The elevators had stopped running, so they went down the stairs three and four at a time. They dashed through the vacant lobby, out the front door, and along the short court that led out

onto the Strand. There they turned left and
headed for a fire lieutenant directing his men
at work trying to put out the fire in the bomb-hit
building. Dave grabbed him by the arm, and
pointed up.

"There are some people trapped on the fourth
floor, sir!" he shouted. "We heard their screams
from our hotel room. Fourth floor, rear."

The fire lieutenant looked at them, saw their
uniforms, and wiped an annoyed look from his
tired face.

"Fourth floor, rear?" he shouted above the
noise of his fire fighting apparatus. "Thought
everybody in that place would be in the shelters.
How many, do you figure? Can't spare any of
my boys, here, so I'll have to go it alone."

"Don't know how many!" Dave shouted back.
"But you're not tackling it alone. We're coming
with you. Let's go."

The fire lieutenant grinned.

"The good old R.A.F. every time!" he cried.
"Right-o! But wait a bit. No sense risking things
bashing you on the head, you know."

The fire lieutenant jumped over to his car in
the street and pulled out a couple of tin helmets.
He tossed them to the boys.

"Put those on!" he shouted. "Right-o! Fourth floor, rear, eh?"

Sticking close to the fire lieutenant's heels, the two boys followed him into the burning building. It was like rushing through the open door of a furnace, and for a second or so the heat seemed almost to knock them off balance. Thick smoke swirled about them like a fog, and the smell of things burning filled their noses and mouths and made them choke and gag for breath.

As though the fire lieutenant had lived in the building all his life, he went straight to the stairs completely hidden by the smoke, and started up. He paused for a second, half turned and stretched out one hand to Dave.

"Give me your hand," he said. "And you take your pal's hand. That way we'll stick together and not get lost. Right you are, now. Up we go!"

There was less smoke on the second floor of the building, and still less on the third. On the third floor, however, they ran straight into trouble. The stair wall had been knocked loose by the exploding bombs, and the stairs were covered by a ton or so of split beams, plaster, brick, and other kinds of debris. The Fire Lieutenant stared at it with a scowl.

"Like climbing the blooming Alps to get over that stuff," he said dubiously. "It might give way under our weight and bury the three of us."

"Look!" Dave suddenly cried, and pointed up toward the fourth floor. "See there on that hall wall? A fire bucket, and a coil of rope. Look, I'll go up and sling down the other end of that rope, after making my end fast. Then you two can work your way up along the rope."

"No, I'll go up!" the fire lieutenant said. "I say—"

Dave was already scrambling spider-like up the debris-piled stairway. With each step forward he seemed to slide back two steps. He'd grab the shattered end of a beam for support, and it would start to pull out and dislodge chunks of plaster and brick. Plaster dust filled his eyes and his throat so that his breath came in rasping gasps. When he was halfway up he heard the fire lieutenant cry out in alarm.

"Watch it, lad!" the man shouted. "That section of wall to your left is starting to go!"

Dave had just time enough to dart a quick glance to his left. A section of wall left standing was bulging out as though a giant were pushing against it from the other side. He took that one quick glance and then scrambled upward for dear life. There was a crash of sound in back of him, and the air was thick with plaster dust. He had flung himself flat on the debris and was clinging to a post of the well railing on the fourth floor by no more than the tips of his fingers.

"Are you all right, Dave?" he heard Freddy's voice from below.

He didn't answer for a couple of seconds. He was too busy pulling himself up onto the solid fourth floor landing. There he turned and looked down through the cloud of plaster dust.

"Made it okay!" he shouted down. "Stand by to receive the line!"

He went over to the fire bucket and took it down off the hook, along with the coil of stout rope. Then, returning to the head of the stairs, he splashed some water down into the cloud of plaster dust.

"Trying to lay that stuff a bit!" he shouted. "Okay! Here comes your end of the rope."

He sent the free end of the coil spinning downward, then knelt down and fastened his end tight about the base of the railing post.

"Got it!" he heard the fire lieutenant's voice, and felt a jerk on the rope at the same time.

At the end of three or four minutes Freddy and the fire lieutenant were on the floor landing with him. The fire lieutenant reached out and squeezed his arm.

"Stout fellow," the man said. "But you're R.A.F., so of course you'd do it. Right-o. This is the fourth floor. The rear, you said? Don't hear a sound. And there doesn't seem to be much fire up here. Guess just the front of this place is burning. Try the doors, lads, but be careful as you push them open. Do it easy like, you know. If the room's burning and the windows are closed, opening the door will be like opening a stove flue. Hold your breath until you're sure. Let's go."

The three of them started down the hall toward the rear, carefully opening doors and glancing into rooms as they went along. Not a light was burning in the building, but the glow of the flames seemed to bounce back from the walls of nearby buildings and light up all the rooms. Dave and Freddy had tried some six or seven rooms when suddenly they looked into a room that made them stop short and catch their breath.

The room was a complete wreck. It was as though that one spot had received the full impact of the exploding bomb. All four walls were completely knocked down. Ribbons of plaster hung from the ceiling, and there weren't any windows, just gaping holes through which streamed the crimson reflection of the flames of another burning building a good two blocks away.

It was not the sight of all that, however, that gave them such a start. It was the sight of the four figures trapped under the pile of debris. Three were men, and one was a woman. Two of the men, and the woman, lay limp and motionless. The fourth man, white with plaster from head to foot, was struggling furiously to wiggle out from under an overturned desk that pinned him to the floor. And all the time he was muttering hoarsely under his breath. He saw Dave and Freddy about the same instant they saw him. He stopped struggling instantly.

"Come in, chaps, and get this blasted thing off my back, will you?" he called out.

Dave waited just long enough to shout to the fire lieutenant and then dashed forward. It took every bit of their combined strength for Freddy and him to lift the desk clear. They succeeded, however, and the pinned man was able to crawl free. He got to his feet and swayed drunkenly. Dave gave him a hand.

"Steady does it, sir," he said. "I'll lead you out into the hall."

The trapped man looked at him out of dazed eyes, mumbled something, and nodded. Dave led him out into the hall and then went back into the room again. Freddy and the fire lieutenant were lifting ceiling and wall beams off the woman. He pitched in and gave them a hand. The woman had an ugly cut on the side of her head, and one arm was obviously broken. She was breathing evenly, however. They placed her in the hall, then went back in for the other two men. Both of them were still alive but badly hurt.

No sooner had they carried the last man out into the hall than there was a rumbling sound like a New York subway train coming along the tunnel to a station. The fire lieutenant let out a yell and grabbed wildly for Dave, who was the last to step out of the room.

"Feared this!" he shouted. "Jump!"

Dave jumped instinctively. Then he started to speak, but didn't. It was not necessary for him to ask the fire lieutenant what it was all about. As he turned, he saw the floor of the room he had just left split straight through the middle from hall door to outer wall. The floor cracked open, and then the two halves dropped downward like the two halves of a hinged trap door. Broken furniture, plaster, brick, and everything else went crashing down into a room on the third floor. The rumbling roar ceased abruptly, and a great column of smoke and plaster dust fountained up from the floor below.

Dave gulped and wiped sweat from his face.

"Gosh, I don't like it that close!" he breathed.

"Great guns!" a voice gasped in his ear. "If you chaps hadn't arrived when you did—Good heavens!"

It was the trapped man they had rescued who spoke. He stood peering through the door opening with eyes that were like dinner plates. Plaster dust still covered him from head to foot, and the red reflection of the flames gave him a weird and eerie appearance.

"Yes, plenty close, sir," Dave said, and then turned to the fire lieutenant. "We'd better get these people down," he said. "Wonder if there are some back stairs here. Have you got stretchers outside?"

"Yes," the fire lieutenant replied. "And there are back stairs, too. I spotted them a minute ago. These people need hospitalization at once. That woman is hurt bad. I'll go down and get help, and take this one chap who can walk along with me. He's had a nasty shock, and I'd better get him out of here. Might go off his topper, or something. You two lads mind watching over the others?"

"No, go ahead," Freddy said for both of them.

The fire lieutenant nodded, then stepped over and took the arm of the plaster-covered man, who still stared glassy-eyed in through the doorway at the collapsed floor. The fire lieutenant spoke, and the man turned and stared at him vacantly. Then his wide eyes wandered over to Freddy and Dave. A strange light glowed in them for a brief instant. He started to open his mouth as though to speak, but closed it slowly, instead. The fire lieutenant tugged on his arm, and then led him along the smoky hallway as he might lead a little child.

"He must have caught a good smack," Dave grunted. "He sure doesn't know what the score is right now. He— My gosh!"

"What's the matter?" Freddy asked quickly. "What's up?"

Dave pointed a finger upward and grinned.

"No guns any more," he said. "The raid's over. Guess you can't hear the All-Clear up here. Gee, do our uniforms look like a couple of wrecks! Wonder if we can get them cleaned at the hotel. Air Vice-Marshal Saunders will heave us out for a couple of bums if we report to him looking like this."

Freddy looked back into the room and gulped.

"And he'll never know how close we came to never reporting to him at all!" he breathed. "Say, I wish that fire lieutenant would hurry up with those stretchers. This woman's coming around a bit. Must be in pretty bad pain. Blast Hitler, anyway!"

"Check!" Dave said grimly. "And if I ever get the chance to *blast* him, how I'll do it, and how I'll love it!"

At that moment the fire lieutenant returned with several of his men. And some fifteen min-

utes after that the three injury cases were safely
in an ambulance that had arrived in the meantime, and on their way to a nearby hospital receiving station. The fire was practically out, and
the heroic soot and grime-smeared firemen were
getting ready to go elsewhere in the city and
continue their valiant work. Guns were silent,
and the long probing beams of the searchlights
no longer pierced the sky. There was not even
the drone of planes in the distance. Death had
come to strike at London, and was now gone.
Behind, it had left more wrecked buildings,
more smouldering ruins, and more dead and
dying. But it had also left behind something
that Adolf Hitler and all of his followers would
never be able to understand, and never be able
to defeat. That was British courage, the superb
fighting courage of the high and the low who
now were fighting on a common ground shoulder to shoulder. London had once again been
hurt, and she was bleeding. But London would
never die, just as England would never die.

Those thoughts trickled through Dave Dawson's brain as he stared up at the flame-tinted
heavens. And once again he was thrilled to the
very depths of his soul to be able to be a part

of all this; to do his share, and fight and fight and fight until the war-thirsty dictators were no more—until they were nothing but an evil and ugly memory.

"I say, you chaps! Blessed if I even know your names. You certainly deserve recognition for tonight's bit. Tell me your names, and I'll see that the Air Ministry hears of what you did."

Dave lowered his gaze to see the fire lieutenant standing at his elbow. He looked at Freddy, and they both shook their heads.

"We're glad we were able to help," Dave said. "Let's let it go at that. You and your men are the real heroes of London, sir. Freddy and I just happened along."

"But that's silly!" the fire lieutenant protested, and wiped his smoke and soot-blackened face with a handkerchief that was just about as black. "This isn't your regular job, you know. And for you two to pitch in and give us a hand, why—"

"Rot!" Freddy grunted. "I was scared pink every second, and know perfectly well I was only in your way."

"Me, too," Dave nodded. "Let's just leave it that way. Where did that chap go—that man you led out?"

"My word, lad!" the fire lieutenant gasped, and looked wildly about. "I'd plain forgotten all about him. Told him to wait and go along to the hospital with the others. Guess he must have wandered off. Well, I must be toddling along. More fires, you know. Good luck, you two. By George, you R.A.F. chaps are certainly right as rain, I say! Well, cheerio!"

"Thumbs up!" the two boys chorused, and watched the fire lieutenant drive off up the street.

When the car had turned the corner of a block, Dave grinned at Freddy.

"Well, shall we make that black-out inspection tour you were yipping about?" he asked.

"The one we've made is enough for tonight!" Freddy grunted. "Besides, we've got to do something about these uniforms, because tomorrow we have to—"

"Yeah, I know," Dave cut in with a worried sigh. "We have to report to Air Vice-Marshal Saunders. Okay, let's see what we can do about these duds, and then hit the hay."

"If Goering's little boys will let us," Freddy murmured as he dropped into step. "And I doubt it very much."

CHAPTER FIVE

Air Vice-Marshal Saunders

THOUGH FREDDY FARMER had his doubts about Goering's "little boys," it so happened that they did not come back to London again that night. Bright and early next morning the two boys were up and inspecting what the hotel's valet service had been able to do about their uniforms. It wasn't a bad job of cleaning, but it wasn't a good job either. True, they would pass muster out at their own squadron, but the Air Ministry, where the Royal Air Force "brass hats" prowl about, was something else again.

"If Air Vice-Marshal Saunders is one of those fussy chaps," Freddy said, and fingered a fire-scorched cuff of his tunic, "he'll probably bleat all over the place."

"Well, what the heck?" Dave cried. "We'll just tell him what happened, and add that we didn't have time to get new uniforms."

"Didn't have the cash, you mean," Freddy said with a grin.

"Same thing, isn't it?" Dave shrugged. "Well, we've got to take our chances, that's all, and hope that he is an okay guy. How do you feel?"

"Stiff as a board," Freddy said, and moved his shoulders. "I feel as if I'd been holding up that building all night."

"Know just what you mean," Dave chuckled. "But you're mistaken."

"Mistaken?" Freddy echoed, and glanced up with a puzzled frown on his good-looking face.

"Sure," Dave said with a nod. "About holding up that building. You only held up half of it. My aching joints tell me I must have been holding up the other half. Well, let's go hunt up some chow. Boy! It's a swell day, anyway— for whatever is going to happen."

Dave moved over to the bomb-shattered window and looked out. There was still a thin pall of smoke hovering over London like a grim reminder of what had happened during the dark hours. On high, however, there was not a cloud to be seen. The sky was a soft blue bathed in the golden rays of the rising sun. When you looked up into that sky, it was hard to believe that death had struck just a few hours before, and that right now it was poised and waiting to strike again when darkness returned.

"What a pip of a day for flying!" Dave breathed softly. "I sure hope Air Vice-Marshal Saunders doesn't keep us hanging around for very long. Me, I want to get back to the squadron and get to work. The Jerries are sure to take a crack at us on a day like this. Boy! This is almost as good as the kind of weather we have back home."

"You mean twice as good," Freddy snorted in his ear. "But hurry up and button your tunic, or you'll be spouting poetry in another couple of minutes. I'm hungry."

Dave sighed and shook his head.

"There's a man for you!" he groaned. "Beauty, war, fire, famine, or flood—they don't mean a thing to him! Only his stomach. Well, you're in for a big surprise, my young fellow.

There's one thing they don't allow in the R.A.F."

"What?" Freddy demanded as they walked out of their room.

"I won't tell you," Dave grunted, and headed for the elevators. "I think I'll let you find out for yourself. But no, you are a pal of mine, aren't you?"

"Oh, come off it!" Freddy growled. "I'll bite. What is this wonderful ruling I don't know about?"

Dave jabbed him in the stomach with his thumb.

"They don't let you wear a corset in the R.A.F., my friend," he said. "So watch how much you eat. Also, you might get stuck the next time some Messerschmitt pilot makes you bail out. A Spitfire's cockpit isn't any too big, you know."

"Indeed I do know," Freddy grunted, and watched the elevator slide up and come to a stop. "And that's something I've been wanting to ask you, Dave."

"Well, then, shoot," Dave said. "I'll always help a pal out with the correct answer."

Freddy didn't speak directly. He waited until they were in the elevator. It contained two men in civilian clothes and two women. Looks of frank admiration were cast their way, but Freddy pretended not to notice. He stared at Dave, and there was a look of baby innocence and curiosity in his eyes.

"You'll really tell me, Dave?" he asked in a voice just a trifle loud. "You'll really give me the answer?"

"Sure," Dave said without thinking. "Just ask me the question. I'll give you the answer. What?"

"It's your legs, Dave," Freddy said. "I've often wondered. They're so confoundedly long and skinny, just what do you do with them in the cockpit of your Hurricane? Is it true that the mechanics have cut holes in the fuselage so's you can let them hang out over the leading edge of the wing? But what about when you're landing? What touches the ground first, your feet or the wheels?"

When Freddy stopped, Dave's ears, neck and face were a bright red, and there was a look of murder in his eyes. Everybody in the elevator was roaring with laughter. It was all he could do to keep from taking Freddy by the throat and throttling him right then and there. However, he could take kidding as well as dish it out, and by the time the elevator had reached the lobby level he was laughing as loud as anybody.

"Okay, pick up the marbles for that one, sonny boy," he said to Freddy as they headed for the breakfast room. "But next time it's my turn. And, boy, look out, what I mean!"

"Don't worry!" Freddy chuckled, and squeezed his arm. "With you around, a chap has to watch out constantly."

All through breakfast they maintained a steady stream of kidding chit-chat talk. Of course each knew what was really uppermost in the other's mind: one Air Vice-Marshal Saunders. Neither of them mentioned it, though, until the meal was over and it was time to go and report at the Air Ministry located but a few blocks from their hotel.

It was Dave who brought the subject up. He slid a tip beside his empty coffee cup, looked at Freddy, and pushed back his chair.

"Well, let's quit stalling and go see what it's all about," he said. "I'm going nuts with worry and wonder, aren't you?"

"Am I!" Freddy breathed, and gave a little shake of his head. "To tell you the truth, I feel exactly like a criminal waiting for the jury to come in with the news of his fate. What do you suppose—?"

"Don't ask!" Dave cut in. "I've been slowly going nuts asking myself the same question over and over again. Oh, heck ..'s go. They can't do any more than sh... us!"

They walked ... short distance to the Air Ministry in mutual thoughtful silence. Just inside the wide front doors of the building, they gave their names, ranks, and squadron numbers to an officer seated at a desk that was practically covered with rows of bell buttons. When they added that they were reporting on orders to Air Vice-Marshal Saunders, the officer shot a scowling glance at their uniforms. He didn't say anything, however. He simply nodded, wrote something on a card and then jabbed a button and picked up a Husho-Phone. A moment later he hung up and stabbed another button. An R.A.F. staff sergeant seemed to pop down out of the air. The non-commissioned officer saluted smartly. The officer at the desk handed him the card.

"Take these two officers to Air Vice-Marshal Saunders," he said in a crisp voice.

The staff sergeant took the card with his left hand, saluted smartly again with his right, and looked at Dave and Freddy. They nodded. The sergeant clicked his heels, executed a smart about-face and went off down the hall. Dave and Freddy followed.

"Holy smoke!" Dave breathed out of the corner of his mouth. "Did you get a load of all the bell buttons on that desk, Freddy? I wonder if he's got one that'll do it? There sure are enough."

"Do what?" Freddy whispered back. "What are you talking about?"

"A button he can jab to make Hitler pop out of a secret door in the wall," Dave chuckled. "Boy, wouldn't it be something if all those connecting wires should get mixed up! I think I could enjoy myself at that officer's desk some quiet night with nobody around."

"I can just imagine!" Freddy grunted. "And what a madhouse this place would be the next morning! Well, forget it, my lad. There's a chap at that desk twenty-four hours a day, I fancy."

Dave glanced back over his shoulder just in

time to see the officer reaching out to punch another button. He sighed heavily.

"It's still a swell idea," he murmured. "Well, we're getting close."

The office of Air Vice-Marshal Saunders was at the rear of the third floor. The sergeant turned the two boys over to a smartly uniformed flight lieutenant in the outer office. A moment or two later the flight lieutenant ushered them into the presence of the high ranking Air Force official. As Dave saluted and looked at the tall, well built figure, a strange sense of relief flooded through him. There wasn't any worry in him any more, only wonder. Air Vice-Marshal Saunders had not reached his position of high responsibility through political pull, nor by knowing the right sort of people. You had o' to glance at the rows of decoration ribbons under his pilot's wings over the left upper pocket of his tunic to know that. There was the red, blue, and red ribbon of the Distinguished Service Order (the D.S.O.). There was the blue and white ribbon of the Distinguished Flying Cross (the D.F.C.). And on that ribbon was the small silver rosette, or bar, which meant that its wearer had performed a feat of air valor for which he had been granted the D.F.C. a second time. There was also the Air Force Cross, and the Mons ribbon, denoting that Saunders had been with that valiant British army that had met the Germans at Mons in 1914, in the First World War. And, of course, there were ribbons to show that he had been decorated by many other governments. No, one look at Air Vice-Marshal Saunders' row of ribbons, and Dave knew that here was a real soldier, a real pilot, and a man who had won and deserved the high position he now held.

The vice-marshal smiled and nodded acceptance of their salute.

"At ease, gentlemen," he said, and pointed to some chairs. "Sit down. We'll have to wait a bit. The colonel is delayed, but he'll be here shortly. Ah! You were in London last night, eh?"

Both boys looked blank for a moment. Then Freddy found his tongue.

"Why—why, yes, sir," he stammered. "But how did you guess, sir?"

"And I'll bet five pounds," the senior officer said with a laugh, "that you two have been worrying yourselves sick that I would hit the ceiling, and rant and rave all over the place, eh?"

"Why, yes—sure—I mean—" Dave stumbled and stopped. "I don't think I understand, sir."

The vice-marshal laughed again and pointed a finger.

"Your uniforms," he said. "Souvenirs from Hitler, I fancy. Did a bomb fall on you, or did you go out hunting for one? Knowing you fighter command lads, I'm guessing it was the latter."

The words banished the last of any fears that might have been lingering in the boys' minds. They relaxed completely and laughed.

"It was about halfway between, sir," Freddy explained. "I mean, a couple of them landed close to the hotel, so—well, we went out and took a look, you might say."

"We didn't bring extra uniforms, sir," Dave added. "And this was the best the hotel could do. I'm sorry, sir."

"Sorry?" the air vice-marshal echoed. "About a little bit of water-soaked and fire-scorched cloth? Rot! It's not the looks of a uniform that really counts; it's what's inside that matters. I won't push you for information, but I fancy you did more than just take a look. I— Ah! There's the colonel now."

The boys heard the door open in back of them. They both got quickly to their feet, turned around, and stopped dead with their eyes popping in sheer amazement. A big man in civilian clothes was walking into the room. He had a strip of surgeon plaster over his left eye, and his left hand was completely hidden by a bandage. He walked with a slight limp. The two boys watched him, speechless. They stared at him as though he were a ghost, because it was the man who had been trapped under the desk in that bomb-blasted building the night before.

"Ah, good morning, Colonel," they heard Air Vice-Marshal Saunders say. "Had a bit of an accident, eh? Or is this just another of Intelligence's disguises?"

"Not this time, sir," the colonel said with a tight smile. "Caught a bit of trouble during that mess last night, and— Well, bless my stars!"

The injured man had looked at Dave and Freddy for the first time. His eyes grew wide with amazement, and he gave a little shake of his head as though to clear his vision.

"Great guns, you two?" he gasped. Then,

turning to Air Vice-Marshal Saunders: "Are these two Pilot Officers Dawson and Farmer—the two I'm supposed to meet?"

"That's right, Colonel Fraser," the air vice-marshal replied. "Why? You've already met them?"

"And jolly well right I have!" the colonel exclaimed. "But for these two chaps, and a fire lieutenant, I wouldn't be here now. I was in my secret office last night with two of my agents, and my secretary, when a bomb caught the place fair and square. We were all trapped under the wreckage. These two lads got us out a split second before the floor gave way and dropped everything down onto the next floor. Great guns, this is a small world. And say, you two, I'm deucedly sorry about last night."

"Sorry, sir?" Dave echoed, and gave him a questioning look.

The man reached up his good hand and touched the strip of plaster over his eye.

"Got a bit of a crack, and it put me off my napper for a spell," he said. "I was pretty much in a daze while you lads were saving our lives. When I came around, I found myself in my regular office in the War Office building. Must have walked all the way there. Everything came back to me clear as day, but you and those fire fighting chaps had left the spot by the time I got back there. But I certainly want to express my heartfelt thanks to you two, now. I certainly owe my life to you."

"We're glad we were of service," Freddy said, as embarrassed crimson seeped up into his cheeks. "How about the others, sir? Are they getting along all right?"

"Coming along fine," the other said. "Miss Trumble, my secretary, will be out of things for a bit, and I'll certainly miss her. Smartest woman in the service. But that's a jolly sight better than losing her completely. By Jove, this is like a cinema thriller, isn't it! My word!"

Dave and Freddy moved their feet uncomfortably and glanced at Air Vice-Marshal Saunders. The high ranking officer was grinning broadly and slowly nodding his head up and down.

"So you simply just went to *take a look,* eh?" he murmured. "Knew perfectly well that it was much more than that. You two certainly have the reputation for chasing after trouble, *and* whipping it." *

The air vice-marshal suddenly stopped short. The smile faded from his face, and he stared gravely at the two young R.A.F. pilots for a moment or two.

"And that is just why you are here," he said presently. "This officer, as you probably have guessed already, is Colonel Fraser, of British Intelligence. He is the one who wishes to speak with you. I only suggested to him that you two should have first chance to listen to what he has to say. Shall we all sit down? Colonel, are you ready to start?"

The Intelligence officer seemed to have difficulty in tearing his eyes from the two boys. He finally succeeded, and nodded. And as though a curtain had been drawn across his face, he too became grave and unsmiling.

"Yes, of course, sir," he said in a flat voice. "Let's get on with it at once."

As Dave sat down on his chair again, his heart was pounding so hard he feared it would push right out through his chest. His throat was dry with excitement, and there was that familiar tingling at the back of his neck. The tingling

* *Dave Dawson at Dunkirk.*

was a sure sign that danger and action were waiting for him just ahead. He glanced at Freddy and saw the look in his pal's eyes. That look said that Freddy was thinking and wondering the same things.

CHAPTER SIX

England Must Never Die

IT WAS A few moments before Colonel Fraser of British Intelligence began talking. He sat staring unseeingly down at his bandaged left hand as though he were choosing the words he would speak. Presently, though, he lifted his head and looked at Dave and Freddy.

"Adolf Hitler's greatest goal in life is to crush the British Empire completely," the Colonel began speaking. "No matter what other battles or minor engagements his troops and his air force may win, they are but steps toward his great goal—the defeat of England. However, in order to defeat England, Hitler must invade and conquer these British Isles. He cannot bring us to our knees from across the Channel. He has got to come over here and beat us into submission. Invasion of England! Those words are on the tongue of every German today."

The colonel paused and pulled a battered pipe from his pocket and a pouch of tobacco. He started to fill the pipe, then stopped and glanced questioningly at Air Vice-Marshal Saunders. The high ranking R.A.F. officer smiled and nodded his head.

"Certainly, Colonel," he said. "Go right ahead and smoke."

The Intelligence officer smiled his thanks for permission and lighted up his pipe.

"Yes, invasion of England is the German password today," he said when the pipe was going. "And ever since Dunkirk and the fall of France the Germans have been preparing for the great attempt. We have been preparing, too—preparing to meet that invasion and throw it back into the Channel. I do not have to tell you of the preparations we have made. You've seen them countless times from the air, and you have no doubt seen them on the ground. Also, like every other man in uniform in England, you both have been constantly on the alert and ready to answer an invasion attempt alarm. Well, the attempt was not made right after Dunkirk. It was not made in the month of July. Nor was it made during the month of August. Why?"

Colonel Fraser paused to tamp down the tobacco in his pipe with a fingertip.

"Why?" he repeated. He shrugged and made a little gesture with his pipe. "I do not know," he said. "No one in England knows. As a matter of fact, I'm quite sure that only Hitler knows. Of course we can guess at a thousand reasons why the attempt has not been made, yet. But it is possible that they might all be wrong. This much we *do* know. It has not been made, yet. And this is something we can also be equally positive is true. The desire to invade and conquer England *has not left Hitler's mind for a single second*. The instant he believes that all is ready, he will give his generals the order to invade us. I mean, by that, to *attempt* to invade us!"

The colonel gave some more attention to his pipe and then continued.

"Naturally, we haven't been so foolish as simply to prepare in every possible way we can, and then sit back and wait for him to strike. The

R.A.F. Bombing Command has been blasting away at Nazi invasion bases on the French, Belgian, and Netherlands coasts night after night, as you both well know. The Navy has been on constant patrol seeking for signs of invasion. It is not known by many people, but we have even done a little invading of our own. Small detachments of sapper troops have slipped ashore in France under the cover of darkness, and made short raids as far inland as Lille. And as you two well know, the R.A.F. has made countless photo and reconnaissance patrols over the occupied countries. And lastly, but by no means least, British Intelligence agents have been sent into the occupied countries, and they have been working day and night, too, in an effort to ferret out scraps of information regarding Hitler's invasion plans. Now!"

The Intelligence officer paused for breath, or perhaps for emphasis.

"Now, this is what I'm leading up to," he said. "The raids we've made, the pictures we've taken, the reports of pilots, and the reports of my own Intelligence agents indicate very strongly that the invasion attempt will be made soon. Perhaps in a couple of weeks, and perhaps in a couple of days. This month, September, the tides and the weather will all be in Hitler's favor. Frankly, I would be willing to stake my life that the attempt will be made sometime this month, but I have no idea whether it will be near the first of the month, or near the last, or even in the middle. That date, however, is something we have absolutely *got to find out*. And that is why I am now speaking to you two chaps."

A quivering sensation like a charge of high voltage electricity shot through Dave. A thousand questions hovered on the tip of his tongue, but he held them in check.

"If there is anything I can do, sir," he said quietly, "I most certainly want to do it."

"And so do I!" Freddy exclaimed with deep feeling. "No matter what it is, sir."

"I told you, Colonel," Air Vice-Marshal Saunders spoke up. "I told you you could count on Dawson and Farmer."

The Intelligence officer seemed not to hear. He sat staring at the two youths. Dave had the strange feeling that the man was staring right into his brain and reading the thoughts there.

'A moment or so later the Colonel gave a short nod of his head and continued.

"No matter what Hitler tries, we'll beat him at it," he said. "If the invasion attempt comes tonight, we're ready, and we'll beat him. That, however, is not the way we want to beat him. We want to beat him *before* he's hardly got started; to smash him *before* he's even come within sight of our shores. In order to do that, though, *we must know the exact date set for the attempt.* That date can be learned. In fact, I almost learned it one day last week. I didn't because a German Messerschmitt pilot shot down and killed the man who was bringing that information back here to me in England!"

The colonel suddenly stopped and seemed to have trouble with his throat. He swallowed a couple of times, then half turned and shot a faint frowning glance at Air Vice-Marshal Saunders. Dave looked at the R.A.F. officer just in time to catch the glint of deep sympathy and feeling that flickered through his eyes. Then Colonel Fraser went on speaking again.

"I spoke of sending my Intelligence agents to the occupied countries. Well, some of them have been there since the war started. A few of them have been there all their lives—were born there, in fact. Intelligence and Secret Service agents are not always recognized citizens of the country they serve, you know. The agent of whom I speak now is a Belgian. All during the last war he fought side by side with British soldiers to free his country from Germany's grip. He is too old to fight as a soldier in this war, but he is fighting again to free his country from Germany's iron grip—Hitler's iron grip. He is doing his fighting in the dark and under cover, but more often than not that kind of fighting is more dangerous than fighting in the open. Every second of the day and night his life is in danger. He never knows when the hand of the German Gestapo may drop on his shoulder. He does not even expect the courtesy of being captured as a spy, in fact. He fully expects to be shot in the back the moment the Nazis realize who he is. But that constant danger does not stop him fighting for one single instant. He loves Belgium, the real Belgium, and he will gladly give his life to help England free Belgium of the Nazi chains of indescribable tyranny. I could talk all day of the things that man has already done for England's cause, but I won't.

Just let me say that he has done enough to win the Victoria Cross a dozen times over."

The colonel took a moment to light his pipe, which had gone out. He puffed smoke toward the ceiling, and smiled faintly.

"That man has gathered more valuable information for me," he said, "than the whole British Intelligence Service put together. And, strange as it may sound, I have never met him personally. I hope some day to have that great honor, but somehow I rather doubt that I will. Anyway, he is the one man who can tell us when the invasion attempt will be made. Now, wait! I can tell from the expression that just this instant came into your faces, that you're wondering why he hasn't sent the information along to me. Well, he has tried to, several times. The last time was only last week. However, though I hate the very thought of the Nazis, I do not consider them as blind, stupid fools. They are ruthless and barbaric, but they are also very brainy, and are cunning and fiendishly clever beyond words. Naturally, they wish to keep their invasion attempt date a secret just as much as we wish to find it out. And so they are leaving no stone unturned to see that it remains a secret. To give it to you straight from the shoulder, five of my best agents have contacted this Belgian, but not one of them has returned to England alive. Every one has been caught in the invisible web the Nazis have thrown about Europe."

A cold lump suddenly formed in Dave's stomach, but he sat perfectly motionless and kept his eyes on Colonel Fraser's face. After a moment the cold lump gradually disappeared. He could guess now why he and Freddy had been summoned to Air Vice-Marshal Saunders' office. There was a job to be done—a job with danger and death constantly hovering about. But after the first start the truth had given him, he no longer felt fright or even slight uneasiness. He felt only the desire to serve humanity and civilization to the last ounce of his strength, and to the last drop of his blood. If the world and civilization went down under Hitler's heel, then life would not be worth the living. He felt that way as he returned the colonel's steady gaze. And the quiet rigidity of Freddy sitting in the chair next to his told him that his English pal felt exactly the same way.

"I can see you two are getting the point," Colonel Fraser suddenly shot at them. "I want to be fair with you, so I ask you this question. Do you want me to continue, or would you rather return to active duty at your squadron?"

"We want you to continue, sir," Dave said, speaking for himself and Freddy.

"Yes, quite," Freddy added. "What can we do to serve, sir?"

The Intelligence officer smiled briefly; then his face became hard and stern, and there was a ringing note in his voice as he spoke.

"There is only one way in and out of Europe, today," he said. "That's by air. This Belgian I spoke of lives in Antwerp. The address is Sixteen Rue Chartres. That street is down by the docks on the right bank of the Scheldt River. He was a marine engineer in his day, and the last I knew he was working for the Germans occupying the city, doing the odd jobs his age would permit. He is close to seventy. He is blind in one eye, and he is not over five feet six inches tall. His hair is grey, of course, and he has a beard. All this I'm saying I'll repeat in detail later. I'm just running over it briefly, now, to give you some picture of the man I hope you can find. Not only hope, but *pray* you will find.

"But to get on with this: I am convinced that

it is sheer suicide for any of my agents to try and contact this Belgian. Antwerp, like every other occupied city of importance, is policed day and night by the Gestapo and German counter-espionage agents. Therefore a man would create suspicion no matter how well he might be established in the city. And remember, I said the only way in *and* out is by air. This highly important job has got to be tackled by one or more pilots. Now—and don't take offense, you chaps —a couple of *Belgian peasant boys* would be less likely to be noticed by the Germans than grown men. And if those two Belgian peasant boys could *fly a plane,* then so much the better. You follow me, eh?"

"Right with you, sir!" Dave blurted out enthusiastically. "And Freddy and I both happen to speak the languages, too."

Colonel Fraser laughed.

"Don't worry," he chuckled, "I had checked on *that* little detail before I asked the air vice-marshal, here, to send for you. Yes, you both are boys—though doing the job of men, believe me —and you both are pilots, and you both speak the languages that will be necessary. And, perhaps the most important thing, you have the courage and the spirit that will keep you going until the job is done. Let me say right here, though, I can't spread the danger angle too thick. It *is* a mighty dangerous job. To give it to you from the shoulder again, everything will be in the Germans' favor, not in yours. If either of you is caught—well, no power on earth will be able to save you. The Nazis will shoot too quickly for that."

The Intelligence officer stopped speaking in order to let the true meaning of his words sink home.

"We know how to shoot a bit ourselves, sir," Freddy spoke up in a steady voice. "So I guess you might say that evens things up some, you know."

"We'll take our chances against any Nazi with itching trigger fingers," Dave said grimly. "But I suppose you've got a definite plan of action for us, sir? I mean—"

Dave cut himself off as the Intelligence officer nodded his head abruptly.

"Certainly," he said. "As you know, the Bomber Command is making raids deep into Germany night after night. Well, tonight you two will go along in one of our bombers, as passengers, you might say. It will be in a bomber of a formation heading for Berlin. They will head for Berlin on a flight route that will take them close to Antwerp. At a certain point you and Farmer will bail out. You'll be dressed as refugee peasant lads, of course, but as the plane will pass over high, you'll have oxygen masks and chest tanks for the parachute drop. When you land you will bury your parachutes and masks, and make your way to Sixteen Rue Chartres."

Colonel Fraser shrugged and gestured with his pipe, which had long since gone out again.

"That ends the first part of the plan," he continued. "The instant you bail out, you will be on your own. You may even lose touch with each other coming down in the darkness. But *Sixteen Rue Chartres* is your goal. And the man you are to get in touch with is known as Pierre Deschaud. He will give you the information we must have. He knows the date, I'll—I'll stake my life on that. He will give you the information, and he will do what he can to help you get back to England. There are several air fields at Antwerp. That we know, of course, from daily photos we have taken. We also know that two or three squadrons of the German *Luftwaffe* are stationed there. Pierre Deschaud will help you steal one of the planes for your flight back to England."

Colonel Fraser stopped abruptly, got out of his chair and began to pace the room. Suddenly he stopped in front of them.

"Any questions?" he asked.

"Yes, sir," Freddy spoke up before Dave could open his mouth. "There was one thing you didn't mention. We may know who Pierre Deschaud is when we meet him, but how is he to know who *we* are? Isn't there some code word or sign he would recognize? After all, we could be anybody, as far as he's concerned, perhaps even Nazis trying to smoke him out."

The stern look suddenly left Colonel Fraser's face. Beaming, he leaned over and patted Freddy's back.

"Good lad!" he said with sincere feeling. "That's just the question I wanted you to ask. Didn't tell you because I wanted to see if you'd think of bringing it up. Yes, there is a code word. It is Houyet. Remember that. *Houyet!* That's the name of the little village in which Deschaud was born almost seventy years ago.

When he hears you say that, he'll know that you come from me. And now, I've said enough for a while. We'll meet again before tonight and go over every little item in detail. I do, however, want to say this. I am a colonel, and chief of British Intelligence, but it is chaps like you, chaps with your courage, and your will to fight against no matter what odds, who will win this war for England and the rest of the decent part of the world. I salute you for accepting this dangerous mission, and I also salute you because I know in my heart that you will win through. And so, until later in the day, gentlemen."

A minute more and Colonel Fraser had taken his departure. Dave and Freddy stood silently staring at each other; grimly reading each other's thoughts—two separate thoughts that really blended into one. Here was a real chance to serve, and they would not flinch or falter for a single instant.

"Well, Dawson and Farmer," Air Vice-Marshal Saunders suddenly broke the few moments of silence, "England is counting on you again. And like Colonel Fraser, I, too, know that you will come through. I, too, salute you."

Dave's heart looped over with pride as the

vice-marshal clicked his heels and saluted smartly. Dave and Freddy solemnly returned the salute, and their hearts were close to bursting with the thrilling joy of that moment.

"And now," the air vice-marshal said as he lowered his hand, "I want to tell you something that may help if the going should get hard. It's something that proves the trust and belief that Colonel Fraser has in you—something that will make you come through, if only for his sake. You recall he spoke of almost receiving that information last week? Of how the man flying it back to England was trapped and shot down by a Messerschmitt pilot?"

"Yes, sir," Freddy said as Dave nodded.

"That man was only twenty years old," Air Vice-Marshal Saunders said, "just a few years older than you chaps. He could fly a plane, but he couldn't serve in the R.A.F., or in any of the active fighting branches of the service, because of physical reasons. He was part cripple. He tried to serve England as an Intelligence agent. He did valuable work for which his memory will long be honored. He gave all he had, his life, for England. His name was Richard Fraser. He was Colonel Fraser's only son. For his sake, as well as for England, you must succeed."

Dave had to swallow the lump in his throat before he could speak.

"Dick Fraser," he murmured more to himself. "That's a swell name, and I bet he was a swell fellow, too. You bet we'll succeed, sir. If it's the last thing we do, we'll find this Pierre Deschaud and come back with the information England needs."

Freddy Farmer cleared his own throat and nodded vigorously.

"You have our word on that, sir," he said evenly. "We won't let you down. We won't let England down!"

"Amen!" Air Vice-Marshal Saunders whispered softly.

CHAPTER SEVEN

Brave Wings Fly Eastward

NIGHT HAD come again to England—black night and the throbbing drone of Nazi planes winging inland from the shoreline of the Channel; swarm after swarm of Goering's vultures who would blast helpless men, women, and children with their deadly loads of bombs, and then return to their bases and report the great number of hits they had scored upon strictly military objectives.

Standing on the edge of a night-shadowed field several miles north of London, Dave Dawson and Freddy Farmer watched the play of searchlight beams, and the glow of burning buildings in the distance. The sound of the bursting bombs was like the dull rumble of thunder far away. But every now and then when the wind changed slightly, they caught the faint chatter of the machine guns of night-flying Spitfires and Hurricane pilots hunting out the raiders high up in the sky.

For several minutes they had been standing there watching the sight and not speaking. There wasn't anything to say except express the desire to be up there doing their bit along with their R.A.F. comrades. And to express such a wish would have been just a waste of breath. Even though it had suddenly been granted, neither of them would have accepted. They had their own job to do. They had pledged themselves to carry it through to a successful end, and neither of them would turn back now even though he were given the opportunity.

One hour ago they had reported to the squadron leader of this Bombing Command unit. He had of course been informed of the flight they were to make, but only up to the point where they would bail out somewhere close to Antwerp. He had welcomed them gravely, but they had not missed the gleam of quiet admiration in his eye. The squadron leader had introduced them to the pilot and crew of the Wellington bomber in which they would make the flight. Flight arrangements had been quietly discussed, and they had been supplied with parachute packs, and oxygen masks and tanks. That done with, the pilots and crews scheduled to make the raid had retired to the Ready-Room for last minute instructions, leaving Freddy and Dave to discuss last minute items between themselves.

There had been nothing for them to discuss, however. Every possible angle of their coming venture had been hashed over and over during a second meeting with Colonel Fraser and Air Vice-Marshal Saunders. A detailed picture of Pierre Deschaud was stamped in their brains. They had poured over a detailed map of the Scheldt River waterfront until they knew it by heart. Every little thing that might help, Colonel Fraser had told them. Ten times, no, a hundred times, they had gone carefully over the whole thing from beginning to end. There was nothing for them to discuss between themselves, now. There was nothing to do but wait until the four plane flight of Wellington bombers, powered by twin 1000 horsepower Bristol "Pegasus" engines, was ready to take off.

"I bet those guys are busting to ask us a million questions," Dave eventually broke the silence between them. "You could see it in their eyes when we were introduced."

"Well, you certainly can't blame them," Freddy replied with a chuckle. "Just look at these duds we're wearing. And by the by, you certainly won't break any girl's heart as a Belgian peasant boy, my pal. Frankly, you look a sight."

"Listen to who's talking!" Dave snorted. "That dizzy-looking get-up of yours is the one thing that has me worried about this flight."

"Ah, so the chap *is* worried!" Freddy murmured. "I thought so!"

"Darn tooting!" Dave said. "One look at you and both of the Pegasus engines on the bus are liable to up and stop working just like that. And then where'll we be? See what I mean?"

"I doubt if they'll even get us off the ground if you get close to them!" Freddy scoffed. "So be sure and stay well back out of sight. But to be serious, Dave, what do you really think of our chances? Oh, I know we'll go the limit, but what do you really think?"

Dave didn't answer for a moment. He turned

his back to the scene of night aerial warfare to the south and stared unseeingly at the four "Wellies" with their propellers slowly ticking over.

"That's a tough question, Freddy," he finally said. "To tell you the truth, I really don't know just what I *do* think. As a matter of fact— No, skip that."

"Skip what, Dave?" Freddy prodded earnestly. "What were you going to say? I really want to know."

Dave looked at him and smiled a trifle wryly.

"Maybe I'm getting old too fast, Freddy," he said. "Or maybe I'm just getting too many cockeyed ideas for my age. But from what I've already seen of this war, nothing is absolutely certain. I mean, you can plot and plan how you're going to do a thing until you're blue in the face; get every little thing all set so that it's—well, so that it's in the bag, as we say back home. Then, *zingo!* Something pops up that knocks all your plans completely haywire. And— Oh, nuts! I guess I'm like a kid whistling in the dark."

"And I feel exactly the same," Freddy said quietly. "But go on. What else, Dave?"

"Oh, skip it!" Dave grunted. "Maybe I'm just

getting cold feet at the last minute."

Freddy stepped close to him.

"Would you like me to bash you one, my American pal?" he asked sharply. "Well, just stop talking that way about yourself. Cold feet? What rot! After what I saw you do at the Dunkirk show? Rubbish! No, Dave, don't talk that way to *me*. Now, what else were you going to say?"

Dave grinned and playfully rasped his knuckles across Freddy's jutting chin.

"One in a million, that's you," he said softly. "One in five million, or name any figure. Well, it's the old hunch business working again, if you must know, Freddy. I mean, everything seems too pat, too cut and dried. I've got the hunch that something we couldn't even dream of is going to pop up and dump us into a mess of trouble before we're back in England again."

"And right you are!" Freddy breathed softly. "I have a feeling just like that, myself. Got it first this afternoon, but I didn't say a word for fear the colonel might take it the wrong way. He might have thought I was hedging and trying to back out. You know, make excuses?"

"Nobody would ever think you were trying

to back out of anything!" Dave said loyally. "But what was it that popped into your mind, anyway?"

"Pierre Deschaud," Freddy said.

Dave shot him a puzzled look.

"Huh?" he echoed. "Pierre Deschaud? So what?"

Freddy hesitated a moment and fumbled with the hem of his coarse peasant jacket.

"Sheer rot, probably," he said after a moment. "But a chap is bound to think of things, you know. Colonel Fraser admits that word from Deschaud cannot get through to him except by one of the colonel's agents. He also admits that the last five agents who have gotten in touch with Deschaud have failed to return. They have either disappeared or died, or both. Well, that makes me wonder a lot."

"Well, he said the Nazis were smart and clever guys," Dave pointed out.

"Sure he did," Freddy nodded. "But don't you get the idea, Dave?"

"The old brain has swallowed up so much to-day, it's a blank," Dave confessed. "What are you driving at, anyway?"

"What proof is there that Pierre Deschaud *is*

still alive?" Freddy asked suddenly.

Dave gasped and went back a step as the real significance of the words came home to him.

"Holy catfish!" he eventually breathed. "That *is* a thought, isn't it!"

"And one worth a lot of consideration, too," Freddy nodded. "As I said, it may all be a lot of rot, but chew on this a bit, Dave. It is possible that the Nazis have trapped and caught this Pierre Deschaud, but aren't saying anything about it. Maybe they are using him, or somebody exactly like him, as bait for the colonel's agents. Don't forget, the last five agents were caught!"

Dave swallowed hard and wiped a hand across his forehead, which had become just a wee bit moist—and not from the warmth of the night air, either!

"Gee, you think of the nicest things!" he muttered. "But you could be right as rain, Freddy, and no fooling. We've got to watch our step. And *how* we've got to watch it! Pick up the marbles, Freddy. You've got the old brain, and no fooling! Any other ideas?"

"No, that one's enough," Freddy said grimly. "Yes, we've got to watch our step, but—well—

that is—I mean, it doesn't make any difference, Dave, does it?"

"Any what?" Dave echoed, and stared at him. "You mean, should we call it off? Hey! One more crack like that, and— Oh, just the old kidder, huh?"

Freddy was chuckling as he grabbed Dave's arms.

"I'm sorry, Dave," he said. "I just couldn't pass the opening. Your face looks so funny when you suddenly get mad. Of course I didn't mean a thing, and I apologize."

"Well, that's better!" Dave growled. Then, grinning slowly: "You did have me going for a second, there. I really thought you were serious, you old tease, you! I must be slipping, not to have got wise at once. I— Uh-uh! I guess this is it, pal!"

The last was caused by the approaching figure of the pilot of the Wellington in which they were to fly. The pilot was Flight Lieutenant Wiggins, and though he wore a heavy flying kit, they knew that the D.F.C. ribbon for air gallantry was under the R.A.F. wings on his tunic. He came up, stopped, grinned, and jerked a thumb in the direction of the waiting Wellington bombers.

"Hitler just called," he announced. "Says the weather is perfect over Berlin, and will we please get it over with? So I guess we'd better get along and please the little fellow, what? You ready?"

"And raring," Dave said with a grin.

"Absolutely fed up with standing on the ground," Freddy added.

The flight lieutenant chuckled and gave them both a keen look.

"I say, drop me a line after it's all over, will you?" he suddenly asked as they started walking toward the planes. "You know my name and squadron address. It should reach me right enough."

"A line about what?" Dave asked in an innocent voice.

"Come off it, my lad!" Flight Lieutenant Wiggins snorted. "You know what I mean. The show you two are scheduled to pull off. We've been pulling out our hair wondering what it's all about. That goes for the squadron leader, too. He swears he doesn't know a thing."

"But that's rot!" Freddy exclaimed, and

buckled his helmet strap tight. "Didn't Hitler say he phoned, just now?"

"The blighter didn't say a word, except that the weather was wonderful and would we please get on with it?" Wiggins chuckled.

"Well, there you are!" Freddy cried. "He's just a shy sort of chap, you know. Probably was afraid that you'd pull his leg about it."

"Oh, quite," the flight lieutenant said with a gesture. "But just what would I pull his leg about? Of course, if it's a deep secret, and you've sworn to Winston Churchill not to breath a word, why then—"

"But we thought *everybody* knew!" Dave said in mock surprise. "Hitler's become fed up. And he's mad at Goering, besides. Goering won't lend him any of his medals any more. So Hitler's mad. He wants to come over here and fight in the British army. Well, you could have knocked me down with a feather when King George asked my pal and me to go over there and bring him back."

"So there you are!" Freddy said. "All very simple. Nothing to it, really."

"Sure!" Dave chuckled. "Get a copy of the

London Times tomorrow. There may even be pictures."

"Say, I'll jolly well do that!" Flight Lieutenant Wiggins said with mock excitement. "And some day I'll tell my grandchildren that I shook hands with the two chaps who nurse-maided Adolf Hitler back to England. So I guess I'd better do that, now."

They had reached the side of the nearest Wellington. Flight Lieutenant Wiggins stopped and in turn shook each boy warmly by the hand.

"Happy landings, lads," he said quietly. "Tally-ho, and all that sort of thing, you know. Well, up into her."

A warm and exhilarating glow tingled through Dave and Freddy as they climbed up through the belly door of the Wellington bomber and made their way forward toward the navigator's cubbyhole just in back of the pilot. The kidding with Flight Lieutenant Wiggins had removed a lot of ugly thoughts. That was the old R.A.F. spirit. Perhaps not one of these Wellingtons would return from their dangerous night raids over Germany, but the pilots and the crews didn't talk about that. They didn't even think about it. They were R.A.F., and there was a job to do. And that was that. No fuss and feathers. No back slapping and brass bands. Battling death and beating it at its own game was routine with them, and they took it as such, with a smile and a joke on their lips.

When they were seated on the two small canvas stools, Dave reached over, pressed Freddy's knee and winked at him in the pale glow of the single light bulb fitted to a fuselage bracing strip. Freddy winked back and smiled. A moment later the fuselage light winked out, and there was no light save the pencil beam of the navigator's bulb, and the fused glow of the instrument panel up forward. Flight Lieutenant Wiggins ran up his engines, checked the radio, and then trundled his bomb-loaded ship to the far end of the field and swung it around into the wind.

There he waited with idling engines for the three other planes in the patrol to take up line-astern position. When they were in place and ready, radio orders came from the field's Operations Office for the take-off. Wiggins pushed throttles forward, and the two Pegasus engines roared up in a mighty song of power. The Wellington quivered and trembled for a moment as though it were reluctant to leave the safety of English soil. Then slowly it moved forward down a long line of flares set out on the field. With every revolution of its twin propellers the plane picked up speed. Presently it was bouncing down that line of flares on its wheels with the tail up. A moment or so more and Flight Lieutenant Wiggins pulled back on the controls. The bouncing stopped, and the Wellington went curving up toward the star dotted night sky.

The instant the wheels were clear and the bomber was mounting up toward Heaven, Dave twisted slightly so that he could peek out the navigator's port and down at the shadowy mass that was England falling away from the plane. For one brief instant stark fright streaked through his heart. It passed, and a tight grin came to his lips. He turned his head and looked past Flight Lieutenant Wiggins and through the reinforced glass nose of the plane—and on into the future.

"Pierre Deschaud, here we come!" he whispered softly to himself.

CHAPTER EIGHT

Terror Rides The Night Sky

ENGLAND WAS far behind in the darkness. The altimeter on the instrument board in front of Flight Lieutenant Wiggins said twenty thousand feet. Both Dave and Freddy had long since stuck the oxygen tubes in their mouths, as had also Wiggins and the members of his crew. And whenever their heads felt a bit light they took a suck of the energy-restoring air and instantly felt normal again. Dave had to grin whenever he looked at Freddy and the others. In their helmets and oxygen masks, they looked like a group of crazy creatures from Mars.

Presently they ran into a bit of weather. The plane heaved slightly, but Wiggins kept it dead on its course. After another bit of time they ran into high clouds. Dave saw Flight Lieutenant Wiggins speaking into his radio mike and knew that the pilot was ordering the other planes of the patrol to spread out so as to avoid collision while flying blind. The nodding of Wiggins' head indicated that the other pilots were acknowledging the order and obeying it.

For some fifteen minutes the plane flew blind through the clouds, then came out into clear air again. Wiggins and the navigator checked their position. Then Wiggins scribbled something on a piece of paper and handed it back to the two boys. They glanced at the short message, which read:

"Tired of looking at your funny faces.
Time to make sure your 'chute packs
are strapped on tight. You will probably
need them on the way down!! Cheeri-o!"

Dave and Freddy grinned at each other, then impulsively they clasped hands warmly. No words were spoken. No words needed to be spoken. They would have been empty and meaningless. The firm pressure of the other's hand had told each far, far more than mere words.

The first part of their venture was quickly drawing to a close. In a short time they would dive away from the droning Wellington into the black night that shrouded German-occupied Belgium. In a few minutes—

But fate, perhaps, had suddenly decided not to let it be that way. Above the drone of the twin Pegasus engines cames a sharp staccato yammer that made fingers of ice clutch at Dave's heartstrings. An instant later he heard the loud voice of the gunner in the tail.

"A couple of the beggers have picked us out!" he cried. "There go the blinking Paul Prys!"

At that moment the Wellington flew straight into a world of brilliant white light. Nazi searchlights on the ground, or Paul Prys, as the boys of the R.A.F. called them, had picked up the Wellington formation in their revealing glare. Instinctively Dave and Freddy grabbed hold of fuselage girders for support. And not a moment too soon, either. Flight Lieutenant Wiggins had shoved the control stick forward and was dropping the Wellington down into a roaring power dive. A couple of split seconds after he started the dive, he sent the plane careening crazily off to the left. The craft roared out of the searchlight beams and plowed away through black night.

"Sweet going!" Dave heard his own voice shout in praise. "That's showing the guys how good their Paul Prys are. Oh-oh! I had forgotten about those birds!"

The last exclamation was caused by the staccato yammer of aerial machine gun fire coming to his ears once again. And almost instantly the sound of the guns in the tail of the Wellington was added to the chatter. Dave and Freddy hugged their seats and felt very helpless and useless. They were really passengers aboard the plane, and there was nothing they could do but sit tight. Sit tight—and think.

That was the hard part. Thinking! Because their thoughts were far from joyous ones. Dave's hunch had started to come true. In another few moments they should have been floating down toward Belgium soil. But all that was changed, now. Fate had guided night flying German planes to their position in the sky, and those Nazi pilots were doing their utmost to finish them off right then and there.

"Just as though they knew we were coming, and were hiding in the bushes!" Dave muttered to himself as British and German aerial machine guns hammered away at each other. "Just as though—Ye Gods! Could that be true? Do the Nazis know that Freddy and I are—"

He cut off the startling thought short and gulped. Then suddenly the whole night sky seemed to explode right on the tip of the Wellington's nose. Colored light and sound raced back to crash against Dave and Freddy as though they were things actually made of solid substances. Dave braced himself and squinted forward. What he saw brought a sharp cry to his lips, and he came up off his stool as though a coiled spring had been released under him.

"We're hit, Freddy!" he shouted over his shoulder. "Wiggins and the other chap caught some of that anti-aircraft shell."

Twisting past the navigator's cubbyhole, Dave went forward to where Flight Lieutenant Wiggins sat slumped over against the controls. His weight had forced the Dep control stick forward, and the Wellington was now tearing down in a thundering dive. The second pilot had been knocked clean off his canvas seat and was stretched out motionless on the cockpit flooring. Bracing himself, Dave reached out and pulled the unconscious Wiggins back in the seat with one hand. Holding the man there, he reached down and grabbed hold of the Dep wheel and gave it all of his strength. The nose tried to drag itself down to the vertical, but Dave's pull on the stick was too much. Inch by inch the plane's nose came up, and after what seemed like years the craft was climbing upward at a slightly flat angle.

"Help me get Wiggins out of the seat!" Dave shouted to Freddy at his elbow. "I'll take over while you fellows see if they're badly hurt."

"Right you are!" Freddy called out in a clear steady voice. "Here, I'll give you a hand with Wiggins and this other chap."

Together the boys lifted and dragged Flight Lieutenant Wiggins and his second pilot out of the cockpit and back toward the navigator's cubbyhole. The navigator seemed too amazed to lend a hand at first.

"But who'll fly the bus, now?" he gasped when he finally found his tongue.

"If she handles something like a Hurricane, don't worry!" Dave shouted, and vaulted into the seat vacated by Wiggins.

The searchlights had once again picked up the

Wellington, and Dave had the crazy impression of flying right straight through the sun as he hunched himself over the controls. A world of brilliant, blinding light smote his eyes, and it was filled with the thundering roar of exploding anti-aircraft shells, and the snarling yammer of death-spitting aerial machine guns. Instinct and instinct alone guided Dave's movements as he struggled to wheel and dive that Wellington out of the dazzling white glare. He couldn't even see the instrument panel in front of him, the light was so blinding. However, you don't need eyes to shove the control stick this way and that. Nor do you need eyes to jump on left or right rudder pedal.

Perhaps the designers of the Wellington bomber would have torn out their hair in anguish at the way Dave Dawson booted their brainchild about the searchlight-stabbed sky over Belgium. But Dave didn't give a thought to that. Perhaps he didn't fly it real pretty like. But a twin-engined Wellington loaded with bombs isn't exactly like a swift sleek Hurricane, so what the heck? The idea was to cut away from those fingers of light that pinned them against the heavens, and that was the only idea. How the heck he brought it about didn't matter. That he could do it was what counted.

And he did succeed. Without warning the Wellington sliced right into a wall of darkness. Dave instinctively reached for the throttles to take strain off the howling engines, but he checked his hand, and let the plane roar deeper and deeper into that blessed sea of darkness. Then presently, when he saw the searchlight beams being frantically swung back and forth across the sky far in back of him, he put the ship in a steady climb and twisted around in the seat.

That is, he started to twist around in the seat, but such movement seemed to make the top of his head fly off. In a flash he realized what was wrong. In the excitement his oxygen mask had slipped down off his face and he could not reach the tube with his lips. Night air was pouring through the shattered section of cockpit glass cowling where fragments of shrapnel had struck, and the sensation was akin to a million icy needles pricking the skin of his face and hands. He let go of the controls, adjusted his oxygen mask and sucked the life giving gas into his lungs. In a second or so he was a new man.

He set the controls for level flight, then twisted around in the seat and looked back.

Freddy and the navigator were bending over Wiggins and the second pilot. Even as Dave looked, the flight lieutenant slowly sat up, made a wry face, and put a hand to his head. Dave sighed thankfully.

"Well, he's pretty much okay!" he breathed. "So that's one of them to handle this bus."

He turned forward for a moment to check the instruments, then scrambled out of the seat and went back. Flight Lieutenant Wiggins saw him and smiled thinly.

"Much obliged, old chap," he said, and slowly stood up. "Had a hunch you two knew something about planes. R.A.F., of course."

The flight lieutenant paused and winked.

"But we won't say a word about what we know," he whispered. "Must keep it very hush-hush, what? And, oh yes, I haven't thanked you for saving our blinking hides, have I? Well, I thank you sincerely, and all that sort of thing."

"Forget it," Dave said, and grinned at him. "I was only thinking of my own hide. By the way, how's your pal?"

Dave pointed down at the second pilot, who

was also sitting up and holding his head in his hands.

"Who, Chubby, there?" Wiggins echoed. "Oh, never worry about Chubby when he gets hit on the head. There's nothing inside to hurt, you see. On your feet, Chubby. We've got to coast about a bit, and find out just where the devil we are, and what happened to the rest of the patrol, too. Then we'll let these two gentlemen off at their stop. Come along, lad. After we've landed, I'll let you look at the cut on *my* head."

Wiggins tapped his second pilot playfully on the shoulder, and then went forward and took over the controls. The second pilot got to his feet, looked at Dave and Freddy and shrugged his shoulders in a gesture of despair.

"And to think I could have flown with dozens of other Wellington pilots," he groaned. "But I had to go and pick a heartless beggar like him. Ah me! Such is life in the R.A.F., lads. All work, and not the slightest bit of appreciation from your superiors. Good luck!"

Dave and Freddy laughed as the second pilot slouched wearily forward to his canvas seat. Five minutes later Wiggins had made contact with the rest of his patrol, and had relocated his position. Another ten minutes and Flight Commander Wiggins turned the controls over to his second pilot and came aft to Dave and Freddy. He replied to their questioning glances with a nod.

"Right-o, chaps," he said. "We're at seventeen thousand and about six miles south of Antwerp. Chubby will cut the engines and take her down another couple of thousand. A free fall will take you out of the Paul Prys in case they hear us and start poking around. And many thanks again for saving the ship. Chubby and I will always think kindly of you, very much so. Well, good luck again."

"Don't thank us," Dave said, and jerked his head toward the tail. "Thank your tail gunner for driving off those night flying planes that were potting at you. What about the rest of the patrol? Did you contact them by radio?"

"Oh, sure," Wiggins nodded. "One reports getting a Messerschmitt, too. They've gone on. We'll catch up with them after you chaps have stepped off into space."

"You're continuing the patrol?" Freddy

gasped, and looked forward at the shattered glass of the cockpit cowling.

Flight Lieutenant Wiggins followed his gaze and chuckled.

"Oh, quite," he said. "That hole's nothing. Besides, the night air will keep Chubby awake, you know. The blighter's always falling asleep and making me do all the flying. And also, I couldn't use up gas lugging these bombs all this distance without dropping them where they'll do the most good."

"And I hope every one is a direct hit!" Dave said grimly, making sure that his parachute harness was properly buckled.

"Me too!" Freddy chimed in. "And I'll give you one guess who I hope you hit right on top of the old bean, too!"

"My, my! What a cold-blooded chap!" Flight Lieutenant Wiggins said in pretended horror. "I don't believe he likes the nasty Nazis a single bit. Well, neither do I, for that matter. Right-o, Chubby! Dig the sleep out of your baby blue eyes, and slide us down three thousand. Our guests are leaving us."

The last was shouted forward. Chubby nodded that he had heard and eased back the throttles until the Pegasus engines were just a rumbling murmur. The nose of the Wellington dipped gracefully and the bomber slid gently down through the night sky. Dave and Freddy moved forward to the belly door that the navigator had opened up. There they waited until Chubby had pulled the bomber up out of its glide and was prop plowing along on an even keel. Dave looked at Freddy, and grinned.

"See you, you know where, pal!" he called out. "Watch out you don't float down on a church steeple. Those things are doggone sharp, you know."

"And you watch out, too!" Freddy cried as Dave got down and let his legs hang down through the opening. "And if you get lost, just send me a postcard. I'll come get you. Happy landings!"

"Ditto to you, Freddy!" Dave shouted, and let his body drop down through the belly door.

CHAPTER NINE

In The Enemy's Country

THE INSTANT Dave Dawson dropped away from the belly of the Wellington black night engulfed him from all sides. He let his whole body go limp and relaxed save for the fingers of his right hand, which he kept tightly curled about the rip-cord ring. For a brief moment or so, as his body turned over and over in that sea of darkness, it seemed as though a million invisible hands were grabbing at the Belgian peasant clothes he wore and trying to rip them from his body. Wind whistled shrilling in his ears, and had he not been wearing goggles he knew that his eyelids would be fluttering like loose blinds in a gale of wind.

Then suddenly his falling body reached its maximum rate of falling speed, and the sensation became one of floating on a huge soft black cloud. He knew he was on his back because he could see the stars straight above him. He raced his eyes across the sky to the east and thought he saw the faint flicker of the Wellington's exhaust plumes, but he couldn't tell for sure. He wondered just where in that star-studded sky above him Freddy might be. Had Freddy already jumped? A sudden thought came to him, and a stifled gasp of alarm rose up to his lips. Supposing something had happened so Freddy couldn't quit the bomber? Supposing his parachute harness had caught on something, and propeller wash had wrenched him free, and he was now spinning headlong downward with a damaged and useless parachute flapping out behind? Supposing—?

He groaned aloud at the torturing thoughts and wished with all his heart and soul that he had waited and watched Freddy jump first. Then he would know for sure that Freddy had bailed out all right. But as it was now, perhaps—

"Watch your own step, sap! Are you going to free-fall forever? Pull the rip-cord ring, dope!"

Perhaps he shouted those words aloud, or perhaps they were only spoken in his brain. At any rate he cut off thinking about other things and gave the rip-cord ring a smart jerk. His body dropped earthward for another split second or so. Then suddenly giant hands reached down from above and violently jerked him back up toward the stars. His body spun around like a top and he was forced to gulp for air. Another few seconds and he was dangling feet downward at the ends of the parachute shroud lines and swaying gently back and forth like the pendulum of a clock. He sucked more air into his lungs, cocked his head and looked downward.

All he could see at first was just one great expanse of utter darkness. It was like gazing down into a coal mine at the hour of midnight. There was nothing but darkness and more darkness. Then gradually, as his eyes became better focussed, he saw not just one great expanse of darkness, but more of a collection of shadows. Some shadows were darker than others, and all of them were of different shapes and sizes. Suddenly he spotted a long snake-shaped shadow. It was almost a dark grey, and he knew at once that it was the Campine (or Kempen) Canal that extended eastward from Antwerp.

Reaching up, he grasped hold of the shroud lines, twisted around and glanced toward the north. He saw a faint cluster of lights that must mark Antwerp. And he was pretty sure that he could make out the Scheldt River that served as Antwerp's water outlet to the sea. He relaxed his grip on the shroud lines, returned his gaze to the shadows directly underneath him and silently praised Flight Lieutenant Wiggins' flying and navigating ability. In exact accordance with orders, the British air ace had dumped them out where they would float down to a point not too far from Antwerp, and not too close so that they might be seen.

"Dumped *them* out?" Dave echoed the thought aloud. "Boy, oh boy, do I hope and pray it *is* them! And not just him, meaning yours truly. Freddy, pal, maybe you're right close to me, and perfectly okay, but I sure wish I could see you and be sure. And how! We hit on all six when we work as a team. Alone, I've got a hunch I'd be just a foul ball. So, Freddy—"

He stopped short because his voice suddenly

choked up so that he couldn't speak. He swallowed and clenched his teeth hard.

"Cut the sob stuff, the sentimental junk, Dave!" he told himself savagely. "There's a job to do whether Freddy's right there with you, or not. And he'd feel the same way about it, too. So pull up your socks, chappy, as Freddy would say, and tend strictly to your knitting."

A couple of moments later there was no more time in which to wonder about this and speculate about that. A sudden change in the mess of shadows directly beneath him told him that the ground was close, and coming up fast. Impulsively he brushed one hand across the lenses of his goggles, as though in so doing he might see objects better. Perhaps that did help some. At any rate, a split second later he caught a flash glimpse of a cluster of pointed shadows, shadows that pointed straight up at him! They were the tops of a clump of trees, and he reacted instantly to the realization that flashed through his brain.

He shot up both hands and grabbed hold of the shroud lines on the right and pulled downward with every ounce of his strength. The action "spilled" air from that side of the silk envelope over his head and caused the parachute and his dangling body to slip off to the side. The tree tops were practically touching the soles of his shoes, and he held his breath for fear he had not side-slipped the 'chute in time. A brief split second ticked past into time history, or perhaps it was an entire year. To Dave it seemed an eternity before the tops of the trees moved away from under him. He quickly jackknifed his knees slightly so that he could absorb some of the "landing shock" with his legs, and automatically threw up one arm across his face just in case there were brambles and shrubs down there. And then the ground rose up and smacked him.

White pain shot up through his left leg. Something cracked him in the small of his back. Something else rammed itself against his right shin. And then something entirely different darted out of the darkness and rapped him on the jaw. He saw thousands upon thousands of colored stars dancing around before his eyes. Then suddenly all was dark and peaceful, and very silent . . .

When he next opened his eyes, he found himself staring straight up at a vast expanse of smudgy grey. He had the sensation of looking up at a poorly whitewashed ceiling. Only it wasn't a ceiling at all. It was the sky, and it was a sort of dirty grey because the last of night still lingered and the Goddess of Dawn had not yet wiped the heavens clean with her veil dipped in sunlight.

For a few moments he continued to stare upward, vaguely conscious of the fact that he was lying stretched out on dew-drenched ground, but not caring much about it. Presently a dull pounding in his head awakened memory. He sat up straight, groaned from the effort, and cradled his head in his hands. That stopped the aching considerably. He took his hands away and looked slowly around. It was then he saw what had happened. Fifty yards away was the clump of trees he had missed by a whisker, but two feet from him was a jagged stone wall he had not missed. The silk of his parachute clung to it in shreds, and the shroud lines were wrapped about jutting rocks like a spider's web. He unbuckled the harness about him and got painfully to his feet. His left trousers leg was ripped from the knee down, and there was a nasty scratch where a point of rock had left its mark. The right shoulder of his coarse jacket was also torn. And to top everything off, he was smeared with mud and dirt from head to foot. He looked down at himself and shook his head.

"Gee, if I don't look like a refugee who's been wandering around plenty long," he breathed, "then there just ain't no such animal!"

He straightened up and looked around again. It was rolling farm country on all four sides, but one look told the pitiful story. War had prevented the land from being worked, and acres and acres of ground were simply going to seed. It was not that fact, however, that caused a look of disgust to come into his face. It was the stone wall, which was no more than a hundred yards long and seemed to serve no purpose whatsoever. There was not another stone wall to be seen in any direction.

"That's Dawson luck for you!" he grunted aloud. "The only stone wall for miles around, but me, I'd hit it sure as shooting. Oh well, I could have broken my neck, I suppose. And at least I don't have to dig a hole to bury the stuff."

As he spoke the last, he started gathering up the tangle of parachute harness, shroud lines, and silk. Then, together with the oxygen mask and tank, that had somehow been twisted clear off his face and around so that it hung down his back, he carefully stuffed everything under the bottom of the wall where it undoubtedly would not be discovered for the next hundred years or so. And probably by that time it would be turned into dust, anyway, and be completely unrecognizable.

When Dave straightened up again, a very urgent and very familiar feeling came to him. It struck him square in the stomach. In short, he suddenly realized that he was as hungry as a wolf. For a brief second fright came to him again. But when he stuck his hand inside his shirt he grinned and sighed with relief. Before leaving England, he and Freddy had been supplied with a small compact case of specially prepared emergency rations that would last them several days in a crisis. To make sure he wouldn't lose it, each had strapped the case about his waist under his shirt. Dave's was still there.

He pulled it out, selected a bar of energy-building chocolate and ate it hungrily. He was tempted to attack a second bar, but will-power refused to permit him to do so. He put the case of emergency rations back in place, fixed his direction from the rising sun and set out across the fields toward a small hill a mile or two away. The lingering shadows of night were completely gone when he finally reached the top of the hill and paused to get his breath. A moment or so later he climbed part way up a tree and stared hard and long at the surrounding countryside.

Some five miles to the north lay the southern outskirts of the city of Antwerp, but for the moment he wasn't interested in Antwerp. The land to the east, and west, and in the direction whence he had come, interested him most. He hoped against hope that from his look-out post he might spot a solitary figure making his way across country toward Antwerp, a lone figure dressed in the clothes of a Belgian peasant refugee. In other words, he prayed that the miracle might come to pass—that he might see and recognize Freddy Farmer trudging toward Antwerp.

His prayer was not answered, however, and the miracle did not come to pass. He saw miles and miles of Belgian countryside, but not the slightest sign of anyone who might be Freddy Farmer. Oddly enough, he did not see a single human being; not even a dog, nor a farm animal. Save for the darkish blur to the north that was

Antwerp, he might have been staring across a completely deserted land. Presently he climbed down to the ground and stood there fighting grimly with his thoughts.

His thoughts were like so many dancing demons that whirled around inside his brain and continually jabbed him with the sharp pointed spears they carried. Where was Freddy Farmer? Had he been able to bail out safely? Had he landed safely? Was Freddy dead? Had he landed in some trees, by any chance, and right now might he be lying helpless and crippled only a short distance away?

The thoughts brought tears of helpless rage to Dave's eyes, and it was hard to beat them back. He tried desperately to argue with himself. He tried to point out to that other side of him that it was hours since he and Freddy had stepped off from the Wellington, and that Freddy was probably in Antwerp by now and making his cautious way to their meeting place at Sixteen Rue Chartres. Certainly that was possible. That stone wall had knocked him out for hours, and he was simply late getting started. Sure, Freddy had landed safe as could be and was now in Antwerp waiting for him. Thoughts and arguments!

Thoughts and arguments! They helped one minute, and drove him deeper into the depths of
worried despair the next.

"Well, just standing here won't get you any
of the answers!" he finally grated at himself.
"Get the lead out of your pants and start going
places. Don't stand here all day and mope, you
fathead!"

The words of self-abuse seemed to help a
little. At least they made him angry at his own
momentary weakness. Fists clenched and jaw
set, he wheeled around and went down the north
side of the hill and toward Antwerp. At the end
of half an hour he had reached the first of the
outskirt streets, and still hadn't met a living soul.
Trudging wearily along the street, striving hard
to act like a peasant lad who was completely lost
and homeless, he kept shooting keen glances at
the rows of houses on either side of the street. A
few of the houses bore the marks of the Nazi air
raids which had taken place before the city fell
into enemy hands, but most of them were in
fairly good condition. Yet as Dave peered at the
fronts and saw the drawn curtains, and a
boarded up door here and there, he felt pretty

sure that that section of the city had been evacu-
ated.

Street after street was the same. It was like
looking at the same picture over and over again.
When he paused, he could hear the faint rumble
of sound from the direction of the city's center,
and every now and then a flight of German
planes winged by high overhead. But in the outskirts of the city all was quiet and still. With
each step his wonder grew, and with each step
the fingers of vague worry clutched at him more
and more. For some crazy reason he was
tempted a dozen times to wheel around and re-
trace his steps in a hurry. But Sixteen Rue Chartres was like a magnet that drew him toward it
and refused to let him retreat.

Then suddenly, as he swung around another
corner, a squad of field grey German soldiers
seemed to rise right up out of the sidewalk. A
non-commissioned officer was in charge of them.
He was a big man with a flat and cruel-looking
face. In his right fist he clenched a Luger, and
the muzzle of that Luger was pointed straight
at the pit of Dave's stomach.

"Halt!" the German ordered in a savage snarl.

CHAPTER TEN

Trapped!

A MOMENT OF wild panic gripped Dave Dawson. His first impulse was to spin around and flee for his life. In the nick of time, however, cold logic made him realize the utter senselessness of such a move. He got a quick hold on himself, threw both his hands above his head and faked a display of mortal terror.

"Don't shoot!" he cried in a high shrill voice. "I have done nothing. I am lost, and I am hungry. Please do not shoot, *Herr Kommandant!*"

To be addressed by such a title of high rank seemed obviously to please the German, who held only a corporal's rank. He smiled and puffed out his chest a bit, and holstered his Luger.

"So, another little vagrant swine, eh?" he leered. "Where do you come from, boy? What are you doing in this area of the city where it is forbidden for civilians to go?"

Inwardly Dave longed to lash out with both fists at the flat leering face, but he had more sense than to ask for a bullet from the German corporal's Luger. Instead he played his part to the limit. He blinked and worked his mouth, and looked for all the world as though he were going to burst out in tears.

"I come from the south, *Herr Kommandant*," he said in a whimpering voice. "From Rotselner, near Louvain. Our farm, it was destroyed in the bombardment. I was separated from my family during the evacuation to Brussels. And when— and when—"

Dave purposely stumbled to a stop and gazed pleadingly at the German corporal.

"May I please put my hands down, *Herr Kommandant?*" he whined. "I am very tired. And I have hurt my leg, as you can see. Please?"

The German grunted and nodded his head.

"Put them down, then," he growled. "All you

Belgians are babies about pain, anyway. Well? You went to Brussels? Why did you not stay there instead of coming up here to bother me, eh?"

Dave gestured miserably.

"The city was filled with refugees," he said. "They would not let any more inside the city limits. They turned us away, and ordered us to go elsewhere."

"So?" the German suddenly echoed as a sharp gleam leaped into his beady eyes. "And when was this? Last week, perhaps?"

Dave was expecting some sort of a trap, so he was prepared, and did not plunge headlong into it.

"No, *Herr Kommandant,*" he said, and shook his head. "It was not just last week. It was a long time ago, last June. Ever since then I have been wandering around trying to find my father, and my mother, and my two sisters."

"And probably stealing all the time, eh?" the German snarled at him. "Yes, I know your kind. We come and save your country from the English dogs, and you thank us by stealing everything you can lay your hands on."

"No, no, I have not been stealing, *Herr Kom-*

mandant!" Dave cried wildly. "I have been looking for work—any kind of work so I could earn money to pay for my bed and a little food. But there has not been much work to find."

"You mean you are too lazy!" the German corporal interrupted harshly. "You look big enough to work, but I know that you are simply lazy. All of your kind are lazy. So you decided to come up here to Antwerp and beg off us? You expected us to put food in your dirty mouth?"

"No, *Herr Kommandant!*" Dave protested with a whimper. "Only if I work for it. Yes, I am strong. I am willing to work, but there is so little work to be found these days. Farther south near Malines, I met a very kind German officer. He was in command of a tank division. He told me that his comrades in Antwerp would give me work to do. He said they would be glad to give me work so that I could pay for my bed and my food."

As soon as Dave stopped speaking, he realized that it had been a mistake to add the little lie about meeting a German officer. The corners of the corporal's mouth went down, and sneering disgust glittered in his eyes. He made a movement with his lips as though to spit.

"You were born!" he snapped. "And that was too much, as I see things. Take him away, Fritz!"

The soldier grinned and prodded Dave again with the barrel of his rifle.

"March in front of me!" he shouted. "Down the street. Try to run away and I will shoot you for a wild pig. March!"

White anger blazed up in Dave, but he still had sense enough to hold himself in check. He kept the frightened look on his dirt-smeared face, let his shoulders droop in cringing defeat, and went trudging along the sidewalk in front of the soldier. At the end of the block the soldier stopped him and made him get into the bucket of a sidecar parked around the corner. The soldier slung his rifle over his shoulder by the strap, forked the seat saddle and leered sideways at Dave.

"You will be a wise little boy to keep your hands clasped in your lap!" he barked. "Don't think that you'll have a chance to jump out and escape. You'll be another dead Belgian, if you try that."

"I shall not try to escape," Dave murmured meekly, and kept his eyes on his clasped hands.

"Then that will be good!" the soldier grunted, and kicked the engine of his army motorcycle into life.

Even if Dave had secretly nursed the idea of attempting an escape, he would promptly have abandoned any such idea once the soldier got the motorcycle and sidecar rolling down the street. The German acted little short of a madman. He streaked along like a bolt of lightning and took corners on one wheel. A dozen times, had not Dave grabbed frantically for support, he would have been bounced out on his head to meet with serious injury. It was an even wilder ride than he and Freddy had taken through the blazing bomb-blasted streets of Dunkirk just a few short months before.*

After a two mile ride that brought them straight into the heart of the city, the German braked to a screaming stop in front of a long flat-roofed building. A glance at it indicated that it had probably been used as a storehouse before the outbreak of war. In a way, as Dave learned a few minutes later, it was still being used as a storehouse, a storehouse for civilian prisoners taken by the Nazi troops occupying

* *Dave Dawson at Dunkirk.*

the city!

The soldier marched him in through the front door and past two giant-sized guards. The guards grinned at the soldier and raised their eyebrows questioningly. The soldier laughed harshly and nodded.

"Caught him trying to sneak through the forbidden area," the soldier said, and jerked his head at Dave. "Where is Sergeant Mueller? My corporal says that he will be in later to make a report."

One of the guards pointed at a door on the left.

"In there, and probably sleeping," he said with a mirthless chuckle. "Go and see him, and leave your little playmate with us. We will see that he has the best of care, eh, Hans?"

The other guard laughed and nodded his head vigorously.

"The very best, of course!" he cried. "We shall let him go and talk with some of his friends. Come along, you!"

A big hairy hand shot out and fingers of steel were curled around Dave's arm. He was almost jerked off his feet as the guard yanked him forward. He kept his balance, however, and was led to the far end of the short corridor into which they had entered. There the guard stopped, gave Dave a warning look, and took a ring of keys from his pocket. He selected a key and opened the door in front of him. Then, faster than moving light, he spun around and hit Dave across the back of the neck.

Stars flared up in Dave's brain, and he saw a sea of blurred faces as he went stumbling through the open door. He fell down a short flight of steps and landed hard on his hands and knees on a rough board floor. For a moment he stayed where he was, waiting for his head to clear. Then the hushed murmur of many voices and a cloying cloud of countless human smells brought his head up and made him get to his feet. He found himself in a huge, long room that contained at least a hundred others in as pitiful looking state as himself.

"There's another one of your comrades!" he heard the guard shout just before he slammed the door.

For a moment or two the hundred pairs of eyes searched Dave's face, and his heart ached as he realized why they were doing so. Here was a storehouse filled with war's driftwood, helpless refugees whose families had been either crushed or broken up by the onward rushing machine of war. Each man there was now searching his face and hoping in his heart to recognize a long lost brother, or father, or some other male relative.

Presently though, they dropped their eyes and went on with whatever they had been doing before he had been hurled into their midst. Nobody made any effort to speak to him, and he understood why. They were not shunning him, or anything like that. They were simply letting him alone with his own sorrows, as they wished to be let alone with theirs. What could they speak about, anyway? Each man's story was the same. There was no real difference. Each had been caught up in the toils of war—and here he was.

Dave swallowed the bitterness that rose in his throat and went over and sat down on a long row of hard wood benches that ran along one side of the wall. An old man sitting there, staring unseeingly at the floor, didn't so much as raise his eyes as Dave sat down. Save for the slight movement of his chest, caused by his breathing, he could have been a man dead. Perhaps in a way he was dead, too. His spirit had been killed by the Germans. Only the physical side of his body remained alive.

Dave flashed him a sympathetic glance, started to speak, but thought better of it. After all, what was there that even *he* could say? Certainly nothing that could give good cheer and heart to this poor old man. Then he thought of the case of emergency food still strapped in place about his waist, and his hand moved impulsively toward the inside of his shirt. He checked the movement, however. The old man looked half starved, but so did everybody else in the place. To take out his specially prepared emergency rations would start a riot, at least.

Then, too—and he felt a little ashamed as he thought of it—there was the matter of his own welfare. In a roundabout way he was fighting for these poor helpless derelicts of war, and for that reason among others he was forced to think of himself first. Right now he was in a tough spot. He was locked up in a Nazi detention prison. Perhaps fate had laughed in Freddy's face, too. Perhaps right now he also was eating his heart out in some other prison nearby. Yes, Dave was a Nazi prisoner, and he didn't dare even think of what would happen if he were exposed—if, for example, he were searched and his secret supply of food discovered, or the small compass, and pocket knife, and one or two other little things he had brought along just in case.

Each little article could well mean a short and snappy trial, and then a firing squad. He wasn't a civilian now, as he had been the last time he and Freddy had fallen into German hands. He was a commissioned Pilot Officer in the Royal Air Force. And what was even more important, right now he was a spy, if ever there had been a spy.

And all of that added up to just one thing. He must get out of this place at all costs, and as soon as possible. It was no use now ranting at himself for not having thrown the incriminating articles away before entering the outskirts of the city. Too late for that, now. The main and important thing to concentrate his brain upon was how and when he was going to escape from this place.

He lifted his head and stared about. There were plenty of windows, but they were a good twelve feet from the floor. There were three doors at the rear of the place, but he couldn't see them very well because of the other refugees in the way. He was certain, however, that they must be securely locked or barred. The thought added to his misery, and he groaned aloud.

"It is of no use to complain, my son, even to oneself," a kindly yet sad voice said at his elbow. "It only adds to one's misery."

Dave turned to see watery blue eyes fixed upon him. The old man who had not moved a muscle as he sat down was now turned around and looking at him out of watery blue eyes that held a wealth of sympathy and a world of sorrow in their depths. Dave smiled and shrugged.

"I will try to get used to it," he said. Then, with a little wave of his hand, he asked, "They have been here long? And why are they here?"

The old man sighed heavily and shook his head.

"Some a day," he said. "Some a week or two. And some, like myself, for many months. Why are we here, you ask? For a thousand different reasons. Yet all the same. We are of no use to the Germans who have captured our beautiful city and driven us from our homes. We are only in their way. My son, look at me."

"I am looking at you, sir," Dave said and felt uncomfortable.

"And what do you see?" the other asked with

bitterness in his voice. "An old man. An old, tired, and broken man. Yet, would you believe it, just a year ago I owned one of the finest perfume businesses in Antwerp. Yes, in all Belgium. I was a very rich man. And now, I am a broken old man."

"But there must be some way of getting out of this place," Dave said, and fought to keep the eagerness out of his voice. "There are only a few guards. And—and you could hide out some place in the city."

The old man smiled as though Dave were a little child asking questions about Santa Claus. He reached out a withered hand and patted Dave on the knee.

"We stay here because there is no other place to go," he said in a patient voice. "They at least give us a little food. No, it is not hard to get out of here. Those doors at the rear are not very strong. They could be knocked down without much trouble. But what then? All Antwerp is watched by the Nazis. Could we go to a friend's house? No. He would not dare let us in. Could we find food? No. The Germans have control over everything. They claim they are protecting us, but they are really breaking our spirits, and our bodies. It is all a part of their system. Escape? Of course. But it would be only a matter of hours before one would be caught—caught and shot down in the street like a mad dog. No, my son, I stay here and try to make the best of it. They may kill me, yes, but I shall not give them the satisfaction of my having them forced to do it."

A lump rose in Dave's throat, and near tears were hot against the backs of his eyeballs. He wanted to put his arm about the old man and do what he could to comfort him. But he feared to attract attention. The old man, and the other poor devils, were resigned to their fate. But not he. He knew now that Lady Luck was still hovering close. Escape was possible. Escape was easy, so it seemed. Escape would be his next bit of action. And, please God, the chance to act would come soon.

CHAPTER ELEVEN

Flight From Nazi Guns

How many hours had passed since he had been pitched headlong into this storehouse of unspeakable human misery? Dave asked himself that question for the umpteenth time as he stared at daylight fading beyond the row of windows so far out of reach. In his saner moments he realized the hours couldn't total more than ten or twelve, but the high tension ordeal of living those hours seemed now to make them total a hundred at least.

Twelve hours of waiting, with every nerve and every muscle of his body on fire. Each time the door had opened, and the face of one of those big guards had appeared, his heart had turned to a chunk of ice in his chest for fear that he was to be summoned for further examination. Right after his short talk with the old man, he had wandered about the place, and when no eye was turned his way he had one by one rid himself of the emergency articles he had brought along. He had tossed them in a dark corner, or stuffed them under a bench—any place, just so that he got rid of them.

However, he had not parted with his little case of emergency rations. That he had kept strapped in place inside his shirt. The knowledge that it was there was a curse as well as a balm. If he was searched, the discovery of those emergency rations might be as bad for him as the Germans finding a couple of rifles and a machine gun stuffed down inside his pants. As a matter of fact, a hundred times he had come within an ace of definitely doing something about that ration case. Each time, though, something had stayed his fingers; something had prevented him from throwing his food supply away.

At any rate, he had hung onto it, and so each time a guard had opened the door his heart had stood still and the sweat of fear had oozed out on his forehead. By good luck, or otherwise, the visits of the guard had meant nothing of importance. Once it had been to toss rank-smelling loaves of bread at the starving throng, and to fill the huge water buckets at one end of the room. The other visits had obviously been only to see that the prisoners were still there, and were not rioting among themselves.

During those long torturing hours Dave had spoken with a few of the other imprisoned refugees. Their spirits had been no higher than that of the old man. They were there for begging, for wandering about the streets after dark, for not getting out of the way of some strutting German officer in time, and for a hundred other utterly ridiculous reasons. They were there because they were of no use and were in the way of Nazi domination and oppression. What would happen to them they did not know. And most of them did not care. Life for them was ended—and they were spirit-whipped enough to let it go at that.

As Dave stopped staring at the fading twilight through the windows, and lowered his gaze to the silent mass of broken men about him, he grimly pledged anew to give his very all, if necessary, to rid the world once and forever of such a system of living as Adolf Hitler and his crackedbrained cohorts were striving to force upon all mankind. As long as there was an ounce of strength in his body, or a drop of blood in his veins, he would fight on to undo all the evil wrought and make the world a better place for the millions yet unborn.

Presently he got slowly to his feet and started shuffling along the wall as though he were going for a drink of water from one of the buckets. A drink of water, however, was one thought not even in his mind. The water buckets were near the three rear doors, and during the long hours of waiting he had covertly examined those doors many times. The old man had been indeed right. They were not at all strong. The locks were so rusted and worn with age, and the hinges, too, that they would fall apart in pieces from a single sharp blow.

But what lay beyond those doors? Bit by bit he had found that out, too, by an innocent question here, and an innocent question there, spoken so as not to arouse the slightest bit of curiosity. If his attempt to escape was to be successful it depended upon no one even suspecting that he was going to try. He had to surprise the refugees as well as the guards. And so he had been very careful about the questions he asked. He had learned that in back were low-roofed lumber sheds, though the lumber had long since been carted away to Germany. Some one hundred yards beyond the sheds was swamp ground that led down to the edge of the Scheldt River. To the right and to the left of the sheds were the poorer sections of the city, deserted now, blasted by bombs in the beginning, and seldom patrolled by the Germans. That knowledge had boosted his hopes high. It was almost as though Lady Luck, herself, had planned it to be that way.

Halfway to those rear doors, Dave caught sight of the old man with the watery blue eyes. The poor old fellow was trying to stretch out on one of the benches rather than suffer the cold of the floor as most of the others were doing, for there were no cots or anything like that. Seeing that old man was like a knife stabbing Dave's heart. He knew that he was foolish to do so, but he did it just the same. He slipped a hand inside his shirt, took one of the specially prepared chocolate bars from his ration case, and palmed it in his hand.

Then he moved over close to the old man.

Watery blue eyes stared up at him, and thin lips made an effort to smile.

"It is not a comfortable bed, my son," the old fellow said in an apologetic voice, "but you will find it less cold than trying to sleep on the floor."

Dave smiled and leaned over so that his body hid his hand from the others. Quickly he slipped the bar of chocolate into a pocket of the old man's tattered coat. He frowned sharply as questions lighted up the watery blue eyes.

"Don't move!" he said in a low whisper. "When you can see me no more, put your hand in your pocket. But do not let the others see you do it. Good luck, my old one."

Before the old man could speak, Dave had straightened up and moved away. In another few seconds he was some ten feet in front of the center one of the three doors. Fading twilight seeped through the cracks—the fading twilight of freedom outside. Dave steeled himself and sucked air into his lungs. For a sharp instant panic overcame him, and his whole body trembled. He beat down his terror, took a quick look around, and then lunged straight for the door. He crashed against it half bent over, shoulders bunched, like an All-American halfback blocking out a particularly dangerous tackler.

The aged door groaned and creaked in protest, and for one horrible moment Dave feared that it would not give way. He had charged it with battering ram force, however. The hinges snapped off, the door sagged, and then it split straight down the middle and went crashing down onto the ground outside. Dave tripped over something and fell sprawling, but he bounced up like a rubber ball and pinned wings to his feet.

Behind him a bedlam of sound broke out. The startled cries of the refugees seemed to pour out through the broken door like flood waters pouring through a broken dam. Dave thought he heard a wild hoarse challenge to halt hurled after him. A split second later the sharp bark of a rifle shot cut above the babble of voices, and something whined past just a little bit above his head. Still crouched over, he darted quickly to the side and sped around the corner of the nearest lumber shed. Halfway down its length, he saw a spot where some of the boards had fallen away, leaving an opening. He swerved and ducked through inside. Slowing his pace a trifle, he cut directly across the floor of the shed and wriggled out through an opening on the other side.

He pulled up to a halt, hugged the shadow cast by the shed and strained his ears. He heard angry voices on the other side of the shed, and the unmistakable sound of pounding feet. He grinned and silently congratulated himself. It had certainly been a bright idea to duck inside the shed. The Germans chasing after him had missed the opening completely and were racing down toward the swamp.

He didn't linger long, though, to congratulate himself on his cleverness. As soon as he got his second wind, he started cutting across lots, hugging the shadows until the lumber sheds were far behind him and he was scurrying along the dark and smelly streets of the deserted poor section of the city. He sneaked along for two or three blocks, then ducked into the pitch dark entrance of a building and paused to rest.

His breath was like fire in his lungs, and every square inch of his body was drenched with sweat. But he grinned happily and his heart sang a song of joy.

"Score one for the good old R.A.F. over Hitler's lads!" he chuckled to himself. "Right through the old line, and how. Boy, what a sensation I'd be in a Rose Bowl game!"

He chuckled a bit more and then snorted at himself.

"Sure, you're a wonderful guy," he grunted derisively. "But you can thank your lucky stars that door was weak. And—"

He cut the rest off short and pulled back deeper into the dark doorway. From up the street came the familiar sound of hobnailed boots on the cobblestones. A second later a harsh order in German hit the early night air.

"Take both sides of the street! Search every house. If you see him, shoot! Shoot on sight! Hurry up!"

Dave gulped and caught his breath. He didn't have to have anybody write him a letter to explain that the Nazi patrols were making a house to house search. Not a bit of it. Perhaps this section wasn't patrolled regularly, but it was most certainly being patrolled now. A grim little game of hide and seek, and one Dave Dawson was *it!*

He inched forward cautiously and peered around the corner of the building entrance.

Some sixty yards up the street were the dim shapes of a dozen or so Nazi soldiers. Each man carried one of those deadly short-barreled rifles which had proved so effective in skirmishing operations. In the center of the street stood an officer. He had drawn his Luger and was waving it around as he barked orders at his men.

One look was enough for Dave. He saw all he wanted to see. He ducked back and slipped inside the house. It was dark as pitch inside, and he was forced to move slowly, feeling the way with his hands and feet. He reached the rear of the building and let himself into a small court. The court connected with the court of a building on the other street. He eased into that building, made his way to the front and peered out. Fate laughed in his face. There were Nazi soldiers in that street, too.

He ducked back inside and grimly considered the situation. He hadn't outsmarted the Germans as much as he had believed. When they hadn't found him among the lumber sheds, they had instantly guessed he had headed for this deserted section of town. In no time extra patrols had been ordered out, and now they were combing the section, methodically searching every house on every street. Even though he ducked from house to house, sooner or later he was going to bump smack into one of those patrols.

"This is what is known as a spot, brother!" he whispered to himself. "Get the old brain working, and get it working fast! There must be some way to fool them. I bet Freddy would think up an idea, just like that."

Freddy! The thought of his pal sent cold shivers of worry slithering down his spine. It seemed ages since he had last heard Freddy's cheerful voice. What he wouldn't give to have Freddy Farmer at his side right now! Would he ever see Freddy again? Where *was* his pal and fighting comrade? What had happened to Freddy Farmer?

He angrily drove the tormenting thoughts from his brain. If he didn't start doing something about himself real soon, he never would see Freddy again—at least, not in this world. At that moment voices not more than three houses away galvanized him into fast action. He spun around and groped back to the rear of the building again and let himself out into the court. There he crouched under some bushes and peered up and down the two rows of buildings.

Every now and then a light would flash in some window, and disappear almost immediately. He watched those flashes of light and listened to the echo of voices moving along the rows of houses.

Suddenly he grinned broadly and hugged himself in delight. There was a perfect way out, and he was a dope not to have realized it sooner. He was sure Freddy would have thought of it right at the start. Sure! The way out was via the courtyards in back of the houses. The German patrols were so busy searching the rooms of the houses, they seemed to have completely forgotten about the courtyards in back. By sneaking along the courtyards, Dave could easily work his way to the rear of houses that the Germans had already searched.

"So get going, before they think of the idea, too!" he ranted at himself.

A little over half an hour later he was crouched in the dark doorway of a house and peering stealthily up the street at the figures of a German patrol moving *away from him*. He watched them until they were lost in the growing darkness. Then he slipped out onto the sidewalk, turned his back on the patrols and headed rapidly in the opposite direction. An hour later he was clear over on the other side of the city and hiding in a group of parked military cars. Tarpaulins had been pegged down over the cars, and he could tell that they had been there for weeks. There wasn't even a lone guard watching over them.

At any rate, it seemed a safe place to hide while he mapped out plans for further action. He was thankful to have slipped safely through the fingers of those patrols hunting him out, but at the same time he regretted that he had been forced to do so. Unless his memory picture of that part of Antwerp was all cockeyed, that detention prison hadn't been more than four or five blocks from Rue Chartres. Had those patrols let him alone, chances were that he would now be close to Number Sixteen Rue Chartres. As things stood, though, he was way over on the other side of the city.

"It's a cinch those patrols haven't given up yet," he pondered the problem to himself. "And ten to one even more patrols have been put on the job. Having a poor refugee give them the slip has probably burned them up plenty. And they're just mad enough to take this whole town apart for the satisfaction of finding me."

He nodded in silent emphasis, and then tackled the problem again. He had the choice of two things, and both were bad. He could start stealing back toward Rue Chartres right now and trust to luck that he would spot Germans wandering about before they spotted him. Or he could wait until daylight, when there would be other civilians on the streets, and take his chances then. Neither idea sounded so hot, but he had to do something.

Suddenly an idea hit him right between the eyes. He grinned, nodded, and silently snapped his fingers.

"Maybe!" he whispered excitedly. "There's just a chance!"

The excitement caused by the sudden thought was so great that for a moment he stood there trembling like a leaf. Then he got a firm grip on his jangling nerves and started thoroughly searching the parked cars. He had searched seven cars before Lady Luck cast her smile upon him. In the eighth car he found what he wanted. It was a staff car and in back was an officer's duffel bag. The bag was covered with dirt and smelled to high heaven, it had been left there so long. Inside the duffel bag Dave found his prize: a spare uniform of the owner, who was perhaps dead or maybe hundreds of miles away. And Lady Luck smiled on him twice, because he discovered with mounting joy that the uniform wasn't a bad fit at all. The service cap was a perfect fit.

Some ten or fifteen minutes later the poor little Belgian peasant refugee had disappeared from the face of the earth. In his place stood a young sub-lieutenant of German infantry. True, his uniform was badly creased, but the crease and the smell of age, Dave hoped, would come out in time. He fumbled through the rest of the duffel bag in the hope of finding the officer's Luger. However, Lady Luck wasn't letting him have everything his own way. There was no Luger, nor anything else that would be of any use.

He grinned and carefully folded his tattered peasant clothes and put them in the duffel bag. Then he fastened the bag tight and put it back exactly where he had found it. Finally he slipped out from under the pegged down tarpaulin.

"Will you get the shock of your life if you ever come back for your spare uniform!" he whispered to some unknown German. "And how, my Jerry lad, *and how!*"

A moment or so later he started to move away from his hiding place, but on second thought he checked himself. The uniform he wore would of course serve as a certain amount of protection, but he would be foolish to stretch his luck. After all, Antwerp was well patrolled at night. There was a curfew law for the civilians, and there was a good chance there was a curfew law for German soldiers and officers, too—for all troops save those assigned to night patrol duty.

"Hold it, pal!" he told himself. "Daylight is your best bet. Then nobody will give you a second look. The streets will be full of troops and officers, then. Right! What's a few more hours of waiting? They might mean the difference between success and a Luger bullet. No, fellow, hold your horses. Play it absolutely safe from here in."

It was hard to slip back in among the parked cars and sit down on a running board, but he forced himself to do it. He'd been receiving too many lucky breaks lately, and he was afraid it would all come to an abrupt end if he didn't watch his step. And so, while every part of him screamed to get into action, he resolutely and doggedly stayed put and waited for dawn.

Just a few hours to wait, but Dave lived his whole life over a hundred times. He thought of everything he had ever done, and recalled hundreds of minor incidents in his life that he was sure he had completely forgotten. He thought of Freddy, and of the R.A.F., and of his friends and relatives back in the States. He thought of everything possible, and played a million games with himself to kill time. But when eventually the light of dawn came oozing up out of the east and the shadows fled westward, and the rooftops of Antwerp began to take definite shape and meaning, his nerves were dangerously close to the breaking point. And it was all he could do to stop himself from leaping to his feet and screaming at the top of his voice, just to do something to let off pent up emotional steam locked within him.

Finally he couldn't stand it any longer. It was still early dawn, but the light was growing brighter all the time. And when he paused and listened intently, he could hear the sounds of the Nazi-occupied city coming to life. He got up off the running board and smoothed out his uniform as best he could. Then he walked nonchalantly out of the parking area and along a street that would lead him in the direction of the river front.

"Here I came again, Pierre Deschaud!" he whispered softly. "And this time I hope it counts!"

CHAPTER TWELVE

Quick Thinking

THE CITY WAS wide awake and getting up steam for a new day of war when Dave finally turned off the main waterfront drive into a winding, shadow-filled lane that was marked Rue Chartres. He paused at the corner and stared hard into the shadows, searching for Number Sixteen. His heart was pounding with excitement, and the blood was throbbing through his veins. Rue Chartres! The end of one trail, and the beginning of another—the air trail that led back to England!

The trip across the occupied city had been absolutely uneventful. He had met groups of Nazi soldiers and had not been stopped once.

As a matter of fact, every soldier he met had
saluted smartly as Dave walked by. Haughty-
eyed, he had returned every salute but inwardly,
he was nearly bursting with laughter. It had
given him quite a kick at first to receive the
salute of Hitler's troops, but after a while it
had become tiresome. From that point on he had
played the stiff-necked German officer to the
limit. He had simply given passing soldiers a
curt nod as a reply to their salutes.

That was all ancient history now. Here he
was at last at Rue Chartres, and somewhere up
that shadowy lane was Number Sixteen and
Pierre Deschaud. He took a step forward and
then hesitated again as the words of Freddy
Farmer flashed by in memory. *Was Pierre
Deschaud still alive?* It was for that reason that
he stopped short and hesitated. Up that street
lay the success or the failure of his dangerous
mission, and for a moment he was almost too
afraid to move forward and find out which it
was.

Thought of the possibility that failure might
be the answer seemed to hold him in an iron
grip and refused to let him move his feet. Then
suddenly a voice cried out harshly off to his

right and along the main waterfront thorough-
fare. He turned to see a German soldier leap
out of a doorway and pounce upon a Belgian
slinking past. The Belgian tried to break away,
but the soldier tripped him up and then hit him
with the barrel of his rifle as the figure fell to
the ground.

In that split second the whole world seemed
to explode inside Dave's head. A red film
dropped down over his eyes, and his whole body
trembled with berserk rage. The sprawled figure whom the German now covered with his
rifle was none other than Freddy Farmer!

Dave's first impulse was to race forward and
hurl himself at the soldier, but he managed to
check the crazy urge in the nick of time. Though
his heart was trying to crash right out through
his ribs, he slowly turned and sauntered calmly
up the street. As he walked along, he shot quick
glances in all directions, and heaved a sigh of
relief when he saw that there was nobody else
about. He quickened his pace slightly and came
to a stop a couple of feet from the soldier who
was standing straddle-legged with his back to
him.

"What's all this?" Dave demanded in harsh German.

The soldier jumped as though he had been stuck with a pin, and wheeled around. When he saw Dave's uniform he clicked his heels and saluted with his rifle, then quickly brought the gun to bear again on the prostrate Freddy Farmer.

"I have captured a missing prisoner, *Herr Leutnant,*" the soldier said. "He escaped from the Central Detention Prison. All night long patrols have been searching the city."

Dave grunted and stared down at Freddy. The English youth opened his eyes. They stared blankly back at Dave for a moment, then swift recognition streaked through them. Dave frowned as Freddy unconsciously started to open his mouth. Quickly Freddy closed it and let a look of terror and fright spread across his dirty and sleepy-eyed face. Dave grunted again, and looked at the soldier.

"The Central Detention Prison, eh?" he growled. "Why did he escape? Who let him escape? There are guards there."

"That is true, *Herr Leutnant,*" the soldier gulped. "But I had nothing to do with it. I am stationed at the western barracks. I was called out to help in the hunt. I do not know the details, *Herr Leutnant,* only that he escaped."

"So?" Dave snapped and fixed the soldier with a scornful eye. "So the first Belgian you meet, you decide he is the one, eh?"

The soldier swallowed hastily a couple of times, and a look of worry crept into his eyes.

"We were given a complete description, *Herr Leutnant!*" he said. "This boy wears the same clothes. I was sure that he was the one, the way he was slinking along. And I clubbed him to the sidewalk, *Herr Leutnant,* because he tried to run away from me."

"Yes, that is true," Dave said gravely, and nodded his head. "I saw him try to run away. But these Belgian fools frighten easily, like rabbits. You, there! Get up on your feet! What is your name?"

As Dave barked the last, he glared down at Freddy. The English youth got tremblingly to his feet, clutching his cap between his fingers.

"My name is Henri Duval," Freddy said in hesitant French.

"So?" Dave growled. "And why did you try

to escape? Did you want to be shot? Why did you try to escape, eh?"

Dave put a lot of emphasis into his words and looked hard at Freddy. The other R.A.F. pilot stared back blankly for a moment, then played up to Dave's lead.

"I did not escape from any place, *Herr Leutnant*," he said.

"You live here in Antwerp, of course?" Dave demanded, and made just the slightest sign of a nod with his head.

Freddy caught onto the tip instantly.

"But of course!" he cried. "I live on the other side of the city, on the Rue Troyes. I was on my way home when the soldier stopped me. I came down here early to see if I could buy a little fish. We have not much food at our house."

While Freddy talked, Dave had been watching the German soldier out of the corner of his eye. The man had scowled at first, but little by little a puzzled look had come into his eyes. By the time Freddy had finished, the soldier was wearing a worried look, and was obviously afraid he had made a mistake. Dave turned and gave him a hard stare.

"It looks like your prisoner who escaped has yet to be found," Dave said sternly.

"But perhaps he lies!" the soldier protested weakly. "Perhaps he does not live on Rue Troyes at all."

Dave could have hugged the German for saying those words. They played right into his hand.

"That is quite possible," he said. "Naturally I shall find out if he is lying. I will take him in my own car and go to his house. Give me your name, and the name of your company commander. If this boy tells the truth, we will forget about this little incident. If he has lied, and is the escaped prisoner, I will see that he is returned to the prison. And I shall also see that your *Kommandant* hears of the part you played in recapturing him."

The soldier hesitated a brief instant, but the fear that he might be wrong was too much for him. He didn't dare insist that he accompany this officer.

"Very well, *Herr Leutnant*," he said, and gave Dave his name, and the name of his commanding officer.

Dave nodded gravely, then repeated the

names aloud to indicate that he was making sure he would not forget them. Then he took hold of Freddy's arm.

"Come along with me!" he said sharply. "My car is in the other block. We shall soon find out if you lied to us or not!"

"On my word of honor, I did not lie, *Herr Leutnant!*" Freddy whimpered, and let Dave pull him along.

As they walked along toward the next corner, it was all Dave could do to stop from looking back to see if the soldier was following. He checked the impulse to do so and walked stiff and straight, keeping a tight grip on Freddy's arm.

"You're breaking the blinking thing in two!" he heard Freddy whisper under his breath. "But God bless you, Dave Dawson! That was a jolly close shave."

"Think nothing of it, my little man," Dave shot out of the corner of his mouth. "Any time you get in a jam, just give me a buzz. I'll always be glad to help out a pal. Now, around this corner. Then hold it while I take a look to see if the boy friend is tagging along."

They wheeled around the corner and stopped

dead. Dave flattened himself against the building wall and gingerly stuck one eye around the corner and looked back. The soldier had stopped looking after them, and was turning around to head off in the other direction. Dave let out the air in his lungs and turned to grin at Freddy.

"The boy friend is gone," he said. "Now, we've got to do something about you, pal. We've got to find some place where we can hide out for a spell."

"What do you mean, do something about me?" Freddy asked with a frown. "I—"

"Use your bean!" Dave reprimanded him, and plucked at Freddy's peasant clothes. "In that get-up you'd advertise yourself as much as though you had a brass band following you around. A peasant did escape, see? It was *me*. But we can't stand here and talk. We've got to duck in some place and get you fixed up some how. Darn! I wish I knew this section."

"Oh, you just want a place to hide, eh?" Freddy said in a voice of superior scorn. "Why didn't you say so? Come along. Follow me. And mind those big feet of yours!"

Dave opened his mouth to ask questions, but Freddy had started moving along the narrow street. He traveled half a block, then darted down into an alley still untouched by the light of dawn. It was so dark that ·Dave plowed straight into Freddy's back before he realized that his friend had stopped.

"Clumsy ox, I must say you are!" Freddy grunted, and then softened it with a chuckle. "Here, give me your hand. The going's a bit tricky from here on."

"Hey!" Dave whispered. "Where in—"

"Shut up!" Freddy whispered. "Everything's all right. I know what I'm doing."

Dave checked all other questions and grasped Freddy's hand in the dark. After some ten minutes of climbing over things, and climbing down the other side, and turning this way and that, Dave suddenly found himself in the bare room of a house. Freddy let go of his hand, closed the door through which they had entered, and made a little apologetic gesture with his hands.

"Sorry, sir, there's no furniture," he said. "But I only took the place night before last, you see. And I haven't had time to send a van for my furniture. Now, if you'll just try the floor, sir."

"Cut the comedy!" Dave said gruffly, and

squatted down on the dusty floor. "How come, anyway? What happened to you? And what have you been doing? And how the dickens did you find this place?"

Freddy raised his hand for silence.

"If you'll just close that big mouth of yours, I'll explain," he said. "And though I don't think anybody can hear us here, as the whole place is deserted, let's not shout, anyway."

"You've got something there," Dave said in a much lower tone of voice. "My error. But, gee, it's good to see you again, Freddy! Boy, oh boy, I'll say it is!"

"Rather pleasant meeting you, too," Freddy said, but his ear to ear grin spoke far more than his tongue. "I can jolly well tell you I've been in a fine funk worrying about what could have happened to you. In prison, you say? Not that that isn't a good place for you sometimes. But what in the world happened to you?"

Dave started to ask for Freddy's story first, but he checked himself. He told of his experiences since the moment he had stepped out of the Wellington right up to the present time. He skipped some of the details, but gave a fairly complete account of his movements.

"And now, what about you?" he finished up. "You weren't stopped at all coming through that forbidden area they've got around the city? That sure was something I hadn't even guessed or dreamed about. A neat way to keep a check on people going in and out of the city by land, anyway."

"Typical of German thoroughness," Freddy said dryly. "It didn't even occur to me, either. Fortunately, though, I was luckier than you. I spotted one of the patrols before they spotted me. Besides, it was dark. I came down in a field about two miles from the outskirts of the city. I hid my stuff and started out at once. I slipped through the forbidden area under the cover of darkness. As I said, I spotted the roaming patrol first, and hid under some house steps until they had gone by. It was even more ticklish business getting over here to the waterfront. I fancy I must have ducked in to hide while patrols passed by a couple of hundred times at least. It was just after dawn when I reached the entrance to Rue Chartres."

"And?" Dave questioned eagerly as Freddy paused for breath. "Then what?"

"Then I did some heavy thinking, as you

would say," Freddy said calmly. "Not knowing whether or not Number Sixteen was a trap, I decided to take a good look around. Then, too, I wanted to wait and team up with you before tackling the place. Well, I nosed around as much as I could. I walked past Number Sixteen several times, but you can't see anything through the windows or doors. I don't think they've been cleaned in years."

"But is anybody living there?" Dave asked. "Could you tell? Could you see anybody? Deschaud?"

"Yes, there's somebody there," Freddy nodded. "An old man who *looks* like Pierre Deschaud, and an old woman. I suppose she's his wife. I've seen them several times. Well, all day yesterday I nosed around as much as I dared. Several times, when you still failed to show up, I was almost tempted to go into Number Sixteen. I thought that perhaps you were already there, and that I had missed you somehow. But I didn't go in. There were quite a few troops about yesterday. They came across the river in boats and were streaming through this section of the city all day long. They were Bavarian troops, and there were thousands and thousands of them. I tell you, Dave, something important must be afoot for all those troops to be around. And they all had full war kit, too."

"Boy, my hat's off to you!" Dave grinned. "I get grabbed by the first Germans I meet, but you wander around among thousands of them! You're good, pal, you're good."

"Rot!" Freddy scoffed, but his face lighted up with pleasure. "I was just lucky enough to slip through the forbidden section at the start. Once you're inside the city, it isn't so hard."

"It's plenty hard, now, for guys in peasant clothes!" Dave said grimly. "But go on. Then what?"

"Well, I hung around close to Number Sixteen as much as I dared, but it was just no go trying to slip inside," Freddy said. "Then when they turned the light out last night, and probably went to bed, I gave it up. I came back here and decided that I'd go in there first thing this morning and take my chances. I was on my way there when that blasted beggar jumped on my neck. Man, was I glad when I opened my eyes to see your homely mug glaring down at me!"

"For that crack I should have walked away and left you to your fate!" Dave growled. Then, with a frown: "The old fellow looks like Pierre Deschaud, huh? Did you see anybody else go in there?"

"Not a soul," Freddy said. "And that's what makes me think that we may be in luck—I mean, that Pierre Deschaud is really alive. I didn't see a single German, or Belgian, so much as glance at the place. Anyway, we've got to take a chance, Dave. We've got to contact Deschaud as soon as we can. I'm worried about seeing all those troops yesterday. And maybe you didn't have the chance to notice, but I did. The harbor is filled with all kinds of barges and strange-looking boats."

"For the invasion!" Dave breathed. "Ten to one they've been making them here."

"That's my guess, too," Freddy nodded solemnly. "They could fill them with those troops, and tugs could take them down the river in no time at all. Of course, we may be all wrong. But I can tell you I'm more than a little worried. We've got to get in touch with Pierre Deschaud as soon as possible. Wait a minute."

Freddy suddenly got to his feet and went over to one of the windows. He peered out a moment, and then turned and beckoned to Dave to come over. Dave went over, and Freddy pointed a finger.

"See between those two buildings?" he said. "See the front of that little shop on the opposite side of that street? The one that has a window with a broken pane of glass?"

Dave pressed his face to the glass and stared in the direction Freddy pointed. He looked across some courts at the rear of the buildings on both blocks and down a short alley to the next street. On the opposite side of the street he could see the doorway, and a part of the front of a small shop that hadn't felt a paint brush in a long time. The windows were so dirty from the weather that he couldn't see inside. Some paper or a strip of canvas covered a space where the window glass was three quarters missing.

"Sure, I see it," he said.

"That's Number Sixteen Rue Chartres," Freddy said. "Another bit of luck for me. This place, I mean. When scrounging around early yesterday morning, I noticed that this place was all tumbled down, and not a soul living here. I decided to find a good place to hide in case I had to. Imagine how good I felt when I discovered that if I wished, I could sit here all day and keep an eye on Number Sixteen!"

"Luck, my eye!" Dave grinned, and patted Freddy on the back. "It was using the old bean, and you know it. I bet you'd already spotted that alley going off Rue Chartres and came around on this street to see what was what."

"Well, I was lucky to find this place like it is, anyway," Freddy said with a shrug. "And— Look, somebody has just put on a light over there! He keeps it burning all day long. An oil lamp, I fancy. With the windows that dirty, I fancy he jolly well has to have some sort of a light inside. He's up and about now, Dave! Shall we—"

"Nix!" Dave cut him off short. "Not *we!* Just *me!*"

"I say, Dave—!"

Dave grinned and put up both hands for silence.

"Keep your shirt on, Freddy!" he said. "You're still forgetting about those duds you're wearing. You might not get ten feet before they'd have you by the scruff of the neck. I'll go and— No!"

Freddy blinked and looked startled.

"What's the matter, Dave?" he asked.

Dave didn't answer right away. He scowled and went through the pockets of his uniform. Suddenly his face lighted up with a grin as he pulled out a German one mark piece.

"I guess I was getting a little selfish for a minute, Freddy," he said. "After all, we're in this thing together. Tell you what. We'll toss this coin. Heads you go, tails I go. This uniform will fit either of us."

"Wait a minute," Freddy cut in. "Perhaps we can find some other clothes for me, and then we can both go. I think the two of us should go together, Dave, in case there's trouble."

"Maybe you've got something there," Dave said with a frown. "But I don't know. Maybe it would be best the other way. If the two of us should get caught, that would be bad. The Nazis would darn well see that there wasn't any more escaping. Now, if just one of us goes, then the other fellow can watch from the window here. If something happens, he'll still be free. See what I mean? No, I really think it's bad dope for both of us to contact Deschaud the first time, don't you?"

Freddy pursed his lips in thoughtful silence for a moment, then nodded abruptly.

"Yes, you're right, Dave," he said. "I'll stay here and watch. If you get into trouble, I'll try and figure a way to get you out of it. No, no arguments, now. You found that uniform, and you're already dressed in it. Besides, you look and act just like a Nazi officer. You really do, Dave."

Dave scowled and gave him a searching look. Freddy grinned impishly.

"Oh, I do, do I?" Dave growled. Then, grinning himself: "Okay, Mr. Wise-cracker, I'll take a whirl at it, if you insist."

CHAPTER THIRTEEN

Sixteen Rue Chartres

As DAVE DAWSON strutted German officer style along the sidewalk of Rue Chartres, he had the crazy feeling that he was ten feet tall, twice as wide, and was wearing a uniform made out of striped red and white silk, with a lamp shade for a hat. There were several German soldiers and civilians wandering along the same street, and to tell the truth, not a single person glanced his way. True, the soldiers saluted him as he passed, but they did so automatically with their thoughts obviously on other things. But to Dave's pounding heart, and his tightly drawn nerves, it was as though he were the most conspicuous thing in all Belgium. It made him angry to think such silly thoughts, but that didn't help him any. Every step he took was another moment of tingling tension. And when finally he came abreast of Number Sixteen, his throat was dry as a bone, and little beads of nervous sweat were trickling down his spine.

He paused there and bent over, supposedly to adjust the lacings of his German boots. Instead, though, he took advantage of the moment to glance keen-eyed about to see if anybody was watching him, or if by chance anybody was trailing along behind him. There was not a single sign of anything like that, however. The military and civilian population of that part of Antwerp was going about its business, and leaving one Dave Dawson strictly alone.

Presently he straightened up, got a firm hold on his jumping nerves, and boldly pushed in through the ancient door of Number Sixteen. A bell tinkled somewhere as he stepped inside. Its sound was echoed by the pounding of his heart, but he only clamped down harder on his nerves. He closed the door behind him and looked around. A gasp of amazement almost spilled off his lips. In all his life he had never seen such a mixed up conglomeration of junk.

There wasn't even a suggestion of order about the room. Coils of rope, parts of marine engines, navigation charts, books, boxes, dirty sea clothes, and goodness knows what were scattered over the place. Shelves along the walls were broken and sagging, their contents long since dumped down onto the floor.

A single oil lamp with a smoke-smudged shade was on a table with only three legs. In a chair by the table sat an old man in the most disreputable-looking clothes possible. His face was thin and the features so pointed as to give the whole a hatchet appearance. Shaggy white hair adorned his head, and a dirty grey beard reached down to the second button of the torn shirt he wore. He held a length of rope in his gnarled bony hands, and had obviously been working on it with a splicing spike when Dave entered. Right now he was staring up at Dave out of the brightest, most piercing set of eyes the young R.A.F. pilot had ever looked into in all his life. They were like X-ray eyes that could look right through your brain and count the hairs on the back of your head from a distance of twenty feet.

For a brief instant the two of them locked

glances. Then the old man dropped his rope and splicing spike and got to his feet.

"Good morning, *Herr Leutnant*," he said in flawless German. "Is there something I can do for you this morning?"

Before Dave could reply, a curtain over an opening at the rear of the disordered room was pushed aside, and an old woman, perhaps even more aged than the man, stepped through. Her eyes flew to Dave's uniform, and the corners of her thin mouth tightened, and stark fear flickered in her eyes.

That sudden look of stark fear in the old woman's eyes made Dave's heart leap with hope. He felt sure that this old man was the real Pierre Deschaud. He was sure of it because the old woman's flash of sudden terror told him she was afraid that, as a Nazi officer, he had come there to do them harm—perhaps to take her husband away. He did not jump at that conclusion, however. He was still on mighty ticklish ground. He had to be sure, *really* sure. He took his eyes off the woman and looked again at the man.

"I was with a friend," he said stiffly. "We became separated and I am now hunting him. I was wondering if he came in here."

"No one ever comes in here," the old man said quietly, and kept his burning gaze fixed on Dave's face. "Perhaps if you could describe your friend, *Herr Leutnant,* I will recognize him if he should come in."

Dave shrugged as though he didn't think that very important, but it was simply a movement to cover up the tremendous quiver of excitement that rippled through his body. The moment of moments was now at hand!

"I will probably find him some place outside," he said, and started to turn. "We are leaving soon for Houyet, and I would not like him to be left behind."

Dave glanced at the old man as he spoke the secret code word, but there was not so much as a flicker of the eyelids. Bitter disappointment and a tingling sense of fear crept into Dave's heart. He hesitated a brief instant and then continued turning toward the door. In fact, he had taken a couple of steps when the old man't quiet voice stopped him.

"I am sorry you have lost your comrade, *Herr Leutnant,*" he said. "It is not likely that he will come into a place such as this. I have nothing to sell but my humble services. I was a marine engineer in my day, but that was long ago. You are interested in boats, *Herr Leutnant?*"

Something caused Dave to stop and turn around.

"I have done a little sailing," he said.

"And so have I, but many years ago," the old man said with a sigh. "But I did my design work on big boats. My masterpiece was the Fraser. She was built right here in Antwerp for an American company. She was beautiful."

Fraser! Colonel Fraser! The mention of that name wiped the last of Dave's fears away. His eyes widened with joy, and he started to open his mouth, but a sudden fierce warning look leaped into the eyes of the old man.

"I have never heard of that boat," Dave said. "For me, the most beautiful boats are built in Germany."

"Ah, yes, they build beautiful boats, indeed, in Germany," the aged one said, and started fishing around in the drawer of the table next to him. "The Fraser, of course, was not a big boat like the Bremen or the Europa. But she was a lovely boat. I think I have a picture of her some place. You would please me by looking at it, *Herr Leutnant.* You can spare the time?"

As the old fellow spoke, he shot a quick meaningful glance at Dave. The young R.A.F. ace caught the meaning and shrugged.

"I have a moment to spare," he grunted. "Show me the picture."

"Ah, here it is!" the old fellow said triumphantly, and pulled something from out of the table drawer. "Here, you can see better under the light. This is not a very good picture, but it will give you an idea of what the Fraser looked like."

As the old man spoke, he beckoned Dave over to the table and blew some dust from an old photograph he had taken from the drawer. Dave stepped over and looked down at the picture. It was one of a single funnel cargo steamer, and not a very trim-looking vessel, at that. It was quite short and stubby-looking, and seemed to be riding exceeding high in the water.

"Is she not a beauty, *Herr Leutnant?*" the old man said eagerly, and then suddenly slid a piece of paper over the lower half of the photograph. "She was four thousand tons, and built sturdy as a rock. I myself was aboard on her maiden cruise."

The old man continued talking about the maiden cruise of the funny-looking ship, but Dave wasn't listening. Every ounce of his attention was focussed on the old man's right hand. He held a stubby pencil in his hand and was scribbling on the sheet of paper he had placed over the lower half of the photo which he held in his left hand. Dave's brain was on fire with excitement by the time the man finally finished and he was able to read the message. The message read:

"Take care! Their eyes and ears are all about. One mile west along the river, there is an old coaling wharf. Just beyond is an old river boat half under water. The bow is above water, and there is a hole on the port side. One can wade out to the hole. Meet me inside that hole at nine tonight. Now ask questions about this picture, and then leave this place."

Dave was forced to steel himself for a second or two to make sure he would keep the wild excitement out of his voice. He reached out a finger and pointed at the bow.

"That doesn't look right," he said. "It seems to ride too high. It does not look to me like a comfortable boat in a heavy sea."

As Dave spoke, he quickly took the stubby pencil from the old man's hand, and wrote, "There are two of us," on the slip of paper. The old man nodded, glanced up at him and nodded again.

"Ah, that proves you know about boats, *Herr Leutnant!*" he cried, and nodded some more. "You are quite right. She was not a very good sea boat at first. We had to make some changes. Afterwards she could ride out any kind of a gale. But perhaps this old man is boring you. So I will stop. I hope you find your comrade, *Herr Leutnant.*"

Dave straightened up and went through the motions of smoothing out his uniform.

"He is probably about some place," he grunted, and turned toward the door. Then, on sudden thought, he kicked aside a coil of greasy rope, and turned his head toward the old man. "You have a dirty place here, old man," he said.

"You had better do something about it, or you may get into trouble."

As the old man mumbled apologies and promises, Dave stepped outside and slammed the door behind him. Hot and cold chills were taking turns racing up and down his spine. His first impulse was to take to his heels and race madly back to Freddy with the news. He curbed the impulse, though, and started along the street at an even gait. So Pierre Deschaud *was* alive? He and Freddy were to meet him in secret at nine o'clock that night! What would Deschaud tell them? Did he really have information about a Nazi attempt to invade England? Colonel Fraser had said that he was willing to stake his life that Deschaud knew, but that wasn't proof that Deschaud actually did know. And it was strange, that note Deschaud had written—and, by the way, had made disappear as if by magic as Dave had left. Deschaud had warned him that Nazi ears and eyes were all about. Where? There in Deschaud's place? But that was a crazy thought. Yet he had had the feeling that Deschaud had been scared stiff that he would say something that would be a tip-off to anybody listening near. But could there be Nazi agents in that place?

Dave shivered at the thought and was forced to swallow hard a couple of times. Before he could stop himself, he turned his head and took a quick glance back over his shoulder. However, there still wasn't a single sign of anybody following him. Just the same he increased his pace slightly. A few minutes more and he had crawled and scrambled over the piles of rubble in the alley next to the deserted house where Freddy was waiting, and was walking into the room.

The grin on his face faded, and the words rising to his tongue clogged in his throat. Freddy Farmer wasn't there. The room was completely deserted. Panic gripped Dave, and his first thought was to spin around and beat a quick retreat. Somebody had found out their hiding place. Somebody had sneaked up and grabbed Freddy while he was talking with Pierre Deschaud. And he had walked right back into the trap.

Cold sweat broke out all over his body. His heart became a chunk of ice that slid down toward his boots. His mouth and throat went bone dry and it was desperately hard to breath. Like a man struck dumb, he stood there, unable to move, unable to decide whether to stay or flee. Then suddenly sounds on the other side of the door he had just closed broke the spell. They were the sounds of footsteps. He took one wild look at the windows and saw that escape was impossible in that direction. The room was rather high above the ground. He whirled around and crouched, fists clenched, and his body tensed to spring forward. Come what may, he wasn't going to be taken without a fight, even though he was unarmed.

An instant later the door was opened and Freddy Farmer stepped into the room. He stopped short and gaped pop-eyed at Dave.

"Good grief, Dave!" he gasped. "Are you ill? What a face!"

Dave released air from his lungs in a whistling sound and straightened up slowly. Reaction set in at once, and his legs felt so rubbery he had to put a hand against the wall for support.

"Ill?" he choked out. "Man, oh, man! I'm practically dead from fright right this minute. Gosh, Freddy, where've you been? Jeepers! Did I get a belt when I came back here and found you gone! I thought the Nazis had nabbed you."

Freddy started to laugh, then instantly cut it off short as he saw the look on Dave's face.

"I say, I'm terribly sorry, Dave," he said. "I should have thought of that, but it completely skipped my mind. To tell you the truth, I got to thinking after you left, about my clothes. I can't go out in them, and I certainly can't stay here in this place forever. So I got to thinking about it. Well, you were lucky, so why shouldn't I be lucky, too?"

Freddy stopped and held out a suit of clothes he had flung over his arm. The suit was covered with dust and even raised a cloud as Freddy moved his arm. But it seemed to be in fairly good condition, even though it wasn't exactly 1940 style.

"I stayed at the window until I saw you leave Number Sixteen," Freddy said. "Then I did a bit of scrounging. The Kind Fairy must have been right at my elbow, for in the third room I looked into I found these, in an old box in a closet. Some other clothes were there, too. These looked the best, though. So here we are. But never mind about me. What about Deschaud? You saw him? You talked with him?"

Dave wiped sweat from his brow, heaved another long sigh of relief, and nodded.

"Right," he said. "And it's Deschaud. I'm sure of that. We are to meet him at nine o'clock tonight. Now, cut the questions, pal. Just give me a chance and I'll tell you everything. And while I'm talking, change your clothes. Just looking at that peasant get-up gives me the shivers. Take it off, quick, and ditch it."

While Freddy changed into his new disguise, Dave told detail by detail about his visit with Pierre Deschaud. Freddy didn't interrupt once, but there was a worried look in his eyes by the time Dave had finished.

"I guess it was Deschaud, all right," he said. "But I certainly don't like that 'eyes and ears about' stuff. Do you think he meant the old woman with him?"

"No," Dave said, and shook his head. "She was scared stiff when I walked in. She stood where she could see him writing. And when I left there was a look of hope, not fear, in her eyes. No, I'm positive that she's his wife, or his sister, anyway."

"Nine o'clock tonight, eh?" Freddy murmured as though to himself. "And it isn't nine o'clock in the morning yet. What'll we do in the meantime? Just wait?"

Dave gave him a scornful look.

"Well, we could go call on the Nazi Commandant at the City Hall, and see how he's getting along," he grunted. "I've got two better ideas, though."

"They'd better be!" Freddy said, and gave him a dark scowl. "What two ideas?"

Dave slipped his hand under his German officer's tunic.

"First a bout with our emergency rations," he said. "My stomach's just about decided my throat has been cut. After that, a few hours of shut-eye. I've got a hunch that it won't hurt a bit to stock up on some sleep."

Their glances met and stayed locked for a long minute. Neither spoke, because each knew what was in the other's mind. Nine o'clock that night was their Zero Hour. At nine that night they would learn what they had come through a hundred lurking dangers to find out. Would it be the end, or, as they both hoped and prayed, would it simply be a glorious fulfillment of their mission?

Suddenly Dave grinned and broke the tensed silence.

"And there's another reason why I want some shut-eye, too," he said.

"I don't like that grin," Freddy said cautiously. "But I'll bite. What?"

"If my eyes are closed," Dave said, and backed away a couple of steps, "I won't be able to see that trick suit of clothes you swiped. Boy! Would your girl friend give you the gate if she saw you in that rig. Hot-diggity! Ain't you something the cat dragged in!"

Freddy snorted, then leaned forward and sniffed loudly.

"Why not be honest?" he asked. "That staff car and duffel bag story was just a fib, wasn't it? You really found that Nazi uniform in a garbage can, didn't you?"

CHAPTER·FOURTEEN

Pierre Deschaud Speaks

BLACK NIGHT had again settled down over Europe. Layers of cloud scud and fog completely hit the stars, and to Dave and Freddy, crouched down on a sandy strip of shore not twenty feet from the waters of the Scheldt River, it seemed as though they were the only two people alive in the whole world. All about them was darkness and utter silence. Antwerp was just a darker blot a mile or so to their left. And although by staring hard they could catch the flicker of pin point lights, the city was so dark and still that the little points of light could well have been their imagination playing them tricks.

It was now exactly eight minutes of nine by

Dave's radium dial wrist watch. A little over an hour ago, when the shadows of coming night had begun to fall, they had slipped out of their hiding place and started a roundabout trip to the spot where they now crouched. Death had walked with them every step of the way, waiting and ready to pounce about them both and gobble them up. But Lady Luck had also traveled with them. And although on three occasions they had come very close to stumbling headlong into Nazi black-out patrols, they had avoided them in the nick of time, quickly changed their route and hastened onward. And now they crouched down on the sandy strip of shore and stared hard at the lopsided darker shadow out there in the water. It was the water-logged and half sunk houseboat, and by straining their eyes hard they could just barely make out the jagged hole stove in the bow on the port side.

Presently Dave turned his head and leaned toward Freddy.

"Deschaud said to meet us inside the thing," he whispered in the English youth's ear, "so I guess we'd better get moving. If anybody is around, he certainly is a darn sight quieter than the night. What do you think?"

"Same as you," Freddy whispered back. "We'd better get out there. Only thing we can do. Watch the noise you make wading."

"You're telling me?" Dave echoed with a silent chuckle. "You bet I'll watch out. Sure could use a flashlight, though. Okay, let's go."

The two boys slowly stood up and crept down to the water's edge. For mutual balance and guidance they clasped hands and started wading. The water was cold and the bottom was very muddy, making it doubly hard to keep their balance. Neither of them, however, met with an accident, and eventually they were directly under the gaping hole in the boat's bow. There the water wasn't more than a very few inches above their knees, and it was not difficult to grab hold of the jagged ends of broken hull planks and pull themselves in through the hole.

It was pitch black inside, and everything they touched was wet and slimy. A thousand different kinds of smells struck them in waves. Inch by inch they crawled forward until Dave found a sturdy cross beam that was comparatively dry. He pulled Freddy to it, and together they sat down and turned around so that they could look out the opening toward the shore. For a moment or so it was like staring at a black curtain hung in a room with all the lights out. Bit by bit, though, shadows began to take shape and they were able to make out the exact shoreline and the tree clumps and building rooftops beyond.

"Well, it's up to Deschaud, now," Dave whispered. "Gosh! I sure hope nothing's happened to him! It's ten minutes after nine!"

"I'm thinking the same thoughts," Freddy whispered back. "But you can bet I sure hope they're all wrong. I— *Dave!*"

Freddy had stopped short and gripped Dave's arm, and was pointing his other hand toward the shore. Dave said nothing, for he had already spotted the faint shadow moving slowly along the strip of sandy beach. The shadow suddenly stopped, and then whirled as a second shadow seemed virtually to leap right down out of the black sky. The two shadows merged together and swayed back and forth. Then one of them fell back and down onto the sand. Freddy's fingers were digging like steel barbs into Dave's arm, but he hardly felt the pain. His breath was locked in his lungs, and all the world seemed to stand still as he kept his eyes riveted on the shadowy scene ashore.

After a moment or so, the shadowy figure remaining on its feet bent over and gathered the fallen shadow in its arms and slung it across a shoulder like a wet sack of meal. Then the shadow moved slowly out into the water. Hardly daring to breathe, Dave and Freddy watched the shadow come closer and closer. Presently it was at the opening in the bow. It paused there motionless, and it was all Dave could do to choke back the shout that struggled to rise up in his throat. Then suddenly a tiny needle thin beam of light flashed across his face and went out almost instantly. Then came a hoarse whisper.

"Give me a hand! Help me lift this traitor inside! Quick!"

The two boys moved forward at once, caught hold of the limp form and pulled it inside the hull of the boat. A second or so later and Pierre Deschaud came slithering in like a greased cat.

"Leave him there," he whispered, and touched them lightly on the arms. "He will be a traitor to Belgium no more. Follow me, and be careful how you step. This craft was not built yesterday."

Before either of them could ask a question,

the old man snapped on the needle point of light
again and glided past them as silently as an eel
in a barrel of oil. They silently followed him
deeper into the boat. After a moment or so he
pushed open a small bulkhead door and stepped
into a bare cabin that had eighteen inches of
water on the deck floor. He paused and waited
for them to pass through, then stepped inside
himself and pulled the door shut. There were
two empty bunks fitted to the walls of the cabin
well above the water line. Deschaud gestured
with his light for them to sit on one, while he
sat down on the bunk facing them. Then he held
his light down at the water, which threw back
a faint glow that made it possible for them to
see each other.

It was Freddy who spoke first.

"What about that one in the bow?" he asked.

"We can forget about him," Deschaud said,
and looked at Dave. "He was the reason I was
so scared this morning. He was in the next room,
and listening, of course. The Nazis do not sus-
pect me, but they do not overlook anything,
either. We have many traitors here in Antwerp,
scum who would send their mothers and fathers
to the firing squad for a few extra loaves of

bread from the Nazi brutes. He was one of them. I have known it for a long time, but I did not dare do anything about it. Tonight, it was different, however. I knew that he would report this boat to his Nazi pay-master. There is far more at stake than his rotten life. And so, there is one less traitor in Antwerp "

As the old Belgian finished, he shrugged his shoulders in a gesture as if dismissing the thought. Dave shivered inwardly, and there was a pounding in his head. So it had been true! A traitor, who could have bought about his death by a single word to his Nazi boss, had been lurking in the next room all the time. Thank goodness he had not been such a fool as to ask Deschaud questions right then and there. Thank goodness the brave and courageous old Belgian patriot had warned him before he'd made a damaging slip of the tongue!

"Tell me your story quickly," Pierre Deschaud's voice suddenly broke into his thoughts. "How did you get here? Who sent you? What is it you wish? Were you seen by the Nazis? Were you followed here? Did you meet anybody on the way? Tell me everything quickly; then I will decide if it is best to talk."

Both boys realized instantly that Pierre Deschaud was checking up on them; making sure that it was safe to tell what he knew. After all, he carried his life in his hands twenty-four hours of the day. And when you do that, you have to be sure of everything, no matter how small or trivial. And so the boys told him everything that had happened to them from the time they had stepped in Air Vice-Marshal Saunders' office at the Air Ministry right up to the present moment. Pierre Deschaud watched them closely out of his X-ray eyes. By the time they had finished, the old man had visibly relaxed, and there was an expression of profound admiration on his face.

"The world will long remember the gallant men of the British Royal Air Force," he said in a voice deep with sincere feeling. "And you two well represent that splendid organization. In the air or on the ground, your courage and your fighting spirit are no less. I salute you from the bottom of my heart. All loyal Belgians salute you. Now!"

The old man paused and leaned forward on the edge of the bunk. As he did so, he drew a

folded sheet of dirty paper from under his torn
and oil-smeared shirt.

"I am convinced you come from the great
Colonel Fraser," he said. "Ah, how I admire
that man! How I should like to meet him one
day."

"And he feels the same way about you, sir,"
Freddy spoke up.

The old man smiled, and the warm light of
great joy glowed in his eyes.

"I pray *Le Bon Dieu* will bring that day to
pass," he said softly. "However, it is of the present we speak. Listen carefully, you two. The
Nazis are going to attempt to invade England.
They are going to attempt to set up a bridgehead
on British soil. Not at Dover, or at Hastings, or
at Brighton on the south coast. It is to be made at
a point, a nine mile strip of shoreline, just north
of Harwich on the east coast. And that attempt
will be made on the night of the sixteenth after
a terrific bombardment by the *Luftwaffe* on the
fifteenth."

"The sixteenth?" Dave gasped excitedly.
"Three days from today?"

"That is correct," the Belgian said solemnly.
"But the *Luftwaffe* raids on the fifteenth will be

directed at the *south coast*. It is a trick to make the British believe that an attack will be made there, while actually the attack will be made much further north on the east coast. Close to seventy-five thousand troops will be used in the first attack. If they gain a foothold in England, three times that number will follow."

Dave unconsciously tried to check the question, but it popped right out of his mouth.

"How do you know this to be true?" he asked.

For an instant he expected to see anger flare up in the Belgian's eyes. No such thing happened, however. Pierre Deschaud simply smiled and slowly nodded his white head.

"Naturally, you ask that question," he said quietly. "It is of course strange that I, an old man, should know the one thing the Nazis wish to keep secret. I do know, nevertheless. I have known all about it for over a month."

The old man paused, lifted a bony hand and pointed in the direction of Antwerp harbor.

"The day they first set foot in Antwerp, they started taking charge of every boat in the harbor, as well as every place where boats are made," he said. "Those of us who were not blind or stupid knew at once the reason. They were starting to prepare even then for the coming invasion of England. I have been a marine engineer all my life. I know how to build boats as well as the next man. The Germans needed men to build barges—long high-sided barges that could be powered by Diesel engines taken from tanks and armored cars. They put hundreds of us to work building those boats. I was one of those men, and the Germans soon realized I knew how to build boats. I acted grateful and overjoyed that they had come. I let them know my hatred toward England for starting the war. I played right into their dirty hands at every turn. It is hard on your heart to strike down a friend, a brave soldier, when you hear him say something against the Germans. Many times, though, I was forced to do that. It was hard, terribly hard, but there was nothing else but to act as I did. There was more at stake than the love and affection of a few dear friends. There was Belgium, and Europe, and England—and perhaps the entire Christian world."

Pierre Deschaud stopped talking and brushed a hand across his eyes, which glistened with tears. Dave wanted to reach out and touch him, and so did Freddy. But they didn't move. They knew in their hearts that the brave old man did not want sympathy. He had done his duty, and the knowledge of that was far, far greater than all the sympathy in the world.

"It was hard, yes," he continued after a moment, "but it was something I had to do. I wormed my way into the good graces of my Nazi jailers. They did not know that I spoke and understood German perfectly. Nor did they know I can remember words spoken for the rest of my life. No, it was not so easy as all that. The Germans did not discuss the invasion much They had received their orders from their superiors to keep their mouths shut. However, a word was spoken here, a word was spoken there, and I filed every word in my memory. All dates, all names of towns, all names of boats, and a hundred other little items. Alone, not one of them means a thing, but after weeks of collecting and remembering words spoken, slips of the tongue, I was able to gain complete knowledge of what was planned."

The old man paused again and held up the folded sheet of dirty paper.

"It is all here, written down in detail," he said as triumph rang in his voice. "Every move they plan to make. When, where, and how. Their complete plan. Get this paper back to England, and the Nazi murderers can be given a smashing blow from which they will not recover for a long time. Get this paper back to your superior officers, and Adolf Hitler will think twice about sending his forces against the British Isles. Mark you, smash this attempt, and Hitler will leave England alone and look eastward for new nations to conquer, not westward toward England."

Pierre Deschaud stopped talking and held out the paper. Dave started to reach out his hand for it, then quickly drew it back. He turned to Freddy.

"We're both R.A.F., Freddy," he said. "But you're *England,* too. You carry the paper, and I'll just tag along with you."

Freddy tried to speak, but his throat was too choked up. He pressed Dave's knee hard with one hand, reached out the other and silently accepted the paper.

"There can be no greater friendship than this!" Pierre Deschaud whispered softly.

CHAPTER FIFTEEN

Danger In The Dark

FOR A LONG moment tingling silence settled over the trio. Then Pierre Deschaud made a little gesture with his hands, and broke it.

"And now, the most dangerous part of all," he said, "your safe return to England with that very valuable paper. And you *must* get back. Five other brave men came for the information you now possess, and they died. *You* must not die. If you fail, all is lost. There will not be enough time left for Colonel Fraser to send over another agent to contact me. It is up to you two, now."

The two boys nodded grimly.

"Colonel Fraser spoke of there being a few

military air fields at Antwerp," Dave spoke up. "What is the nearest and best one for us to tackle and try to steal a plane?"

"I will take care of that little matter, too," Pierre Deschaud said. "Were you to try such a thing alone, you would not live ten minutes. That happened to two of those five. Two others were killed before they even reached a field. And the fifth, a fine lad not much older than either of you, was not fast enough. He was shot down to his death before he was out of sight of Antwerp. But you—you *must* get through!"

"Can we get started now?" Dave asked, and nervously clenched and unclenched his fists. "The sooner the better is the way I see it."

"Right you are," Freddy echoed with a nod. Then, looking at Pierre Deschaud: "There's no use wasting time unless we have to."

"But of course not," the Belgian patriot said, and rose to his feet. "We will start at once. Come with me, and be careful how you step."

The old Belgian turned to a door on the side opposite to that through which they had entered. The door stuck a bit, and he was forced to put his shoulder to it hard before it gave way. Admiration for the aged man, and something close to love, stirred in Dave Dawson. Pierre Deschaud might be close to seventy, but he had the strength of two men, and the courage of a brigade.

Deschaud flickered his light forward to reveal rotting bulkheads amidships. The boat was well down by the stern and at a dangerous slant. Halfway along the port side, Dave suddenly made out the shape of a small shallow rowboat. An instant later he noted that the oars were joined and fixed to swivel brackets so that one could row facing the bow instead of facing the stern as is the usual case. The Belgian sloshed through a foot of sluggish water, climbed into the boat, and motioned to them to get in.

"Sit near the bow," he directed. "That makes her ride better for the one who does the rowing. And I will be that one."

The man paused, chuckled softly and patted the side of the boat affectionately with his hand.

"This is one boat in Antwerp that the Nazi pigs know nothing about," he said in a purring voice. "I made her with my own hands years ago. Before the Nazis arrived, I hid her here in this sunken hulk. She has been worth many times her weight in gold to me. To lose her would be like losing my dearest friend. Now, sit steady, for I am about to put out the light. You will hear me moving, but do not be alarmed. I have a secret way to get her into the Scheldt. I remove but two or three loose planks, and we glide through as nice as can be."

"Where are we headed, sir?" Freddy whispered in the darkness.

"Directly across the river from this point," Pierre Deschaud said, "there is one of their military air fields. A mile of the shore is dangerous swamp ground, however; a man who did not know the way could lose himself, and probably drown, before he even realized what had happened. But I have lived in Antwerp almost all of my life. I know that swamp as one knows the palm of his hand. I will lead you through it safely. And when we reached the edge of the field—but we will attend to that matter when we come to it. Now, silence, please. Not even a whisper. They patrol the river all night long in their E-boats. And they have keen ears and eyes, these Nazi sons of the devil. Now, we start."

Dave and Freddy, crouched near the bow of the small craft, could hear Pierre Deschaud moving, and could hear soft grating sounds like boards being rubbed together. A moment later they felt the boat move under them, and a moment after that the darkness was a little less, and a chilly wind blew against their faces. They had slid out of the half sunken houseboat and were now out in the Scheldt River.

Dave's nerves danced and twitched around, and his head felt light from excitement. He slowly turned and stared off into the blackness to his left. He thought he saw a couple of dim lights far away, but he was not sure. Then gradually his eyes became accustomed to the change of shadowy darkness, and he could make out the sprawling dark hulk that was Antwerp, crouching like some motionless monster on the banks of the Scheldt River. He tilted his head and looked up to see that cloud scud and fog still blotted out the stars. At that moment he heard the throbbing drone of unsynchronized German aircraft engines far to the east. He was not sure, but once or twice he thought he also heard the faint *cr-rump* of bursting anti-aircraft shells. However, though he peered hard in that direction, he could not see any flashes of fire in the dark sky.

Then suddenly there was a muffled roar of

sound up the river in the direction of the water-front center of Antwerp, and a long beam of light stabbed out across the water. Pierre Deschaud's command was like a shrill whistle.

"Face down on the bottom of the boat, quickly! Don't move a single muscle. Pray hard they do not catch us in that light!"

Dave and Freddy dropped flat and practically tried to press themselves into the wooden bottom of the boat. Pierre Deschaud also crumpled down instantly. And as the throbbing of a speedboat drew closer and closer, its sound was matched by the wild beating of three hearts in the bottom of that rowboat. Dave clenched his teeth in an effort to ease the terrible strain of just waiting there helplessly for the beam of light to swerve and catch them in its brilliant glow. Each second was a minute, and the fifteen that ticked by while they crouched there motionless were as a lifetime in a world of unforgettable torment and torture. At the end of that time, the German river craft had roared past their position and was streaking farther on downstream. Each of them realized it at the same time, for they all straightened up together.

"Bless *Le Bon Dieu* for saving us that time!"

Pierre Deschaud breathed in a fervent whisper. "That is a trick of theirs. They slide along without lights, and then suddenly switch on the searchlight, and race forward at full speed, hoping to catch some poor devil where they have forbidden him to be. A thousand curses on their souls. We will yet drive the last of them from this part of the world!"

Pierre made a gurgling sound in his throat for emphasis, then fell to on the oars again. He had greased them well, and had it not been for the movement of the boat, Dave wouldn't have been able to tell if the man was rowing or not. There was not so much as a whisper of sound from the oarlocks.

Twice more they were forced to fall flat and hold their breath in fear as a Nazi river patrol boat streaked by. The last time its savage wash caught them amidships and rocked them about like a chip of wood in an angry sea. But they hardly noticed the tossing they received, they were so thankful that they had not been caught in the searchlight's beam. Then suddenly dark shapes rose up on either side of the boat. They glided along between the dark blurs for a few moments, and then the nose of the boat nudged into a muddy bank and came to a stop.

"Don't move!" Pierre Deschaud whispered sharply. "That river was nothing for its dangers. This is the beginning of the difficult business. Sit still, and I will get out first. I know exactly where to step. And if one does not step just so—"

The old Belgian left the rest hanging in midair as an additional warning to the two boys. He moved forward past them and climbed out. A tug or two brought the bow higher up on the mud. Then they heard his whisper again.

"One of you give me your hand, and with your other hand take the hand of your friend," he said. "Do not let go for a single instant. This is most treacherous. Ah, yes, many men are buried here in this swamp. Now, we move very slowly. Put your foot where the man ahead has put his. If you slip and start to fall, do not cry out in alarm. Hold on tight to the hand you grasp."

As Freddy was closer, he grasped Pierre Deschaud's hand and reached the other hand back to grab Dave's. Then, Indian file style, they started to move forward slowly foot by foot. In the distance Dave heard faint sounds, and it was all he could do to keep from lifting his eyes and peering ahead. He did not do so, however, for he would most certainly miss his footing and go pitching off into the deep muddy pools that lined the row of swamp hummocks along which they walked at a snail's pace.

Time and time again Pierre Deschaud turned to the left or the right, but always it was in the general direction whence came the sounds. Dave's eyes smarted from peering down at Freddy's heels so constantly. But he blinked away the pain and kept doggedly onward. Every now and then some swamp animal would plop off a hummock into the water with a splash that sounded like a cannon going off to Dave's strained nerves. And he could tell from the sudden pressure of Freddy's hand gripping his that his pal wasn't enjoying the journey, either.

For well over half an hour the old Belgian led them step by step through the swamp. Then finally they heard him sigh with relief, and a moment after that they felt firm hard ground under their feet. Dave raised his aching head and looked around. He saw nothing but darkness, but he plainly heard the throbbing purr of an aircraft engine in the distance. He stared hard in that direction, only to realize that they were standing at the bottom of a slight slope of ground. The Belgian pulled them close to him.

"Keep hold of hands," he whispered. "And walk as though your shoes were made of feathers. When I stop, you must stop at once. Remember that. If you don't, you will die, my dear young friends."

"How come?" Dave whispered as the Belgian paused for breath. "What's ahead?"

"These Nazis fear sabotage at their fields," Pierre Deschaud replied. "So they have strung a wire fence about the entire area. The wire is charged with high voltage electricity. If you should stumble against it in the dark—you would never know it."

"But how can we get near the planes, then?" Freddy asked.

"Do not worry," the Belgian murmured. "I will take care of that fence. Now, come. Bend over as you walk, so."

Hunched over forward, the trio crept stealthily up the slope and along the flat for some fifty yards. Then suddenly Pierre Deschaud stopped. Freddy and Dave froze in their tracks and peered ahead. Some three feet in front of them,

they could just make out a five strand wire fence
that was about six feet high. Beyond was a field
of tall, waving, sun-scorched grass. And beyond
that was the level expanse of the military flying
field. They could see dark shapes that were the
hangars and other buildings. And far over on
the other side they could see a Heinkel night
bomber in the faint glow of a single flare. Its
prop was ticking over, and shadows walking past
in front of the light indicated that mechanics
were making night repairs. Then Pierre Deschaud whispered.

"Get down flat on your stomachs," he directed,
"one behind the other. Be ready to crawl forward when I say so. Crawl as if you were swim-
ming, but do not lift your elbows. And keep your
heads down. Now, wait just a moment."

As the boys got down flat on the ground,
Pierre Deschaud pulled a forked stick some two
feet long from under his shirt. Then, crouching
down, he hooked the bottom wire of the fence
in the fork part and lifted it upward as high as
he could.

"Now, one at a time worm your way under,"
came his strained whisper. "Keep as close to the
ground as you can. Now, go ahead."

Dave hesitated a fraction of a second, and then started to inch his body forward. He did so by digging his fists and his toes into the ground and shoving. He kept his face so close to the ground that his nose was rubbing along it. Inch by inch he crawled forward, with air locked in his lungs and his heart hammering against his ribs. Just a few inches above him was sudden and terrible death. If Pierre Deschaud's strength should fail! Or if the forked stick should break and the deadly wire sap downward! Or if—

"There, you are through!" he heard Pierre Deschaud's whisper. "Now, turn around and grasp your friend's outstretched hands and pull him under."

Trembling like a leaf, and his body dripping from nervous tension, Dave got up on his hands and knees and swiveled around. Freddy's head and shoulders were already under the wire, and his hands were outstretched. Dave bent down and grabbed them and slowly pulled his pal through to safety. The instant Freddy's feet were clear of the wire, Pierre Deschaud removed the forked stick and let the straining wire snap back into place.

"And now you have only to hide in that grass

and wait until it is almost dawn," they heard him whisper through the wire. "Always just before the dawn they start up all their engines to remove the chill of the night. The nearest plane cannot be more than seventy yards from where you are, now. Wait until the mechanics have started the planes and walked away to let them warm up. Then dash for the nearest plane. The swift fighters are hangared on this side of the field, so you need not worry about having to steal a huge bomber. And so, I leave you now."

The old man's voice faltered for a moment; then he got control of his emotions.

"May God fly with you, my brave friends," he whispered. "It rests with you, now. I must return to my boat and get back across the river before it is light."

"I wish you could go with us, sir," Dave whispered.

"No, although I thank you for the kind thought," Pierre Deschaud whispered. "However, my place is here in Belgium. Here I must stay until I die, fighting as best I can for the liberation of my country. And so, farewell, my courageous friends. May God fly with you!"

Dave blinked to drive away the tears that

filled his eyes. When he opened his eyes again, there was nothing but darkness beyond the charged wire. Pierre Deschaud had gone back to his boat. Dave felt Freddy's hand groping for his. He gripped it and squeezed hard.

CHAPTER SIXTEEN

Wings Of The R.A.F.

WHEN THE NEW dawn was but a faint streak low down in the east, the sound of a hundred airplane engines being kicked into life suddenly shattered the stillness of the surrounding countryside. The two boys lying flat on their stomachs side by side started violently, then looked at each other and grinned.

"This is almost it!" Dave whispered. "Let's start worming closer. We've got to grab a ship before anybody else gets in the air. Here in the grass, we could easily be spotted from the air."

"You're right!" Freddy whispered back. "And I'm sure whoever saw your uniform and

237

my suit would jolly well land at once to find out what was what. Right-o. Forward we go."

Like two human snakes, the boys wiggled forward through the tall grass until they were but a few feet from the edge of the close cut, level flying field. Through the grass ahead they could see the row of Messerschmitt One-Nines, and One-Tens. And as luck would have it, a Messerschmitt One-Ten was the ship nearest them. It was not more than thirty yards away at the most. Dave nudged Freddy and pointed.

"Just what the doctor ordered!" he breathed. "A One-Ten with plenty of room for two. Hot dog! Hoped I'd get a crack at flying a One-Ten some day. Or do you want to do the flying?"

Freddy smiled and shook his head and touched the pocket of his jacket where he kept Pierre Deschaud's detailed report of the Nazi invasion plans.

"The least I can do in return," he said. "Besides, you spoke first. Look! The mechanics have checked the instruments, and are walking away!"

It was true. Mechanics were climbing down out of cockpits and walking along down the tarmac in groups. In a moment or so there wasn't a single man within seventy-five yards of the first Messerschmitt in the line. Dave gripped Freddy's arm, tried to speak, but couldn't get the words out of his throat for a second. Then they came in a muted rush.

"Okay! Let's go! Luck to us both, fellow!"

Quick as a flash, they shot up out of the grass and started running with every ounce of driving power in their legs. It was only some thirty yards to that One-Ten, but Dave felt as though he weren't covering more than a couple of inches of ground with every stride. A thousand torturing thoughts whipped through his brain, and with every stride he expected to hear the yammer and chatter of many machine guns blazing away at him.

Not a single shot was fired, though. And not a single voice cried out in wild alarm, as he reached the tail of the plane and dashed around it toward the long three-man cockpit. Then suddenly a German mechanic seemed to rise right up out of the ground. Obviously he had been making some delayed check on the plane and was only just starting to join his comrades down at the other end of the tarmac. As he saw Dave, blank amazement flashed across his moon-shaped face. Then his eyes seemed to crackle out fire, and his mouth flew open.

Decision and action were one with Dave Dawson. He dived forward the last step and lashed out his right fist, putting every ounce of his strength in the blow. Perhaps the mechanic tried to duck, but at any rate he didn't do it in time. Dave's driving fist caught him flush on the jaw. His head snapped back, his feet left the ground, and he did a beautiful backward somersault to crash down on the tarmac in a heap. Before the German had even hit, Dave was in the pilot's pit, reaching for the control stick and throttles.

He kicked off the wheel brakes with his foot and jerked his head around. Freddy was already in and grinning from ear to ear.

"The beggar will sleep for a week!" he cried. "Right-o! Give her the gun!"

As though Freddy's voice was some kind of a signal to the Germans about the field, shots suddenly rang out, and the air shivered with shouting angry voices. Dave shoved the throttles forward and the twin 1,150 hp. Daimler-Benz engines thundered up in a mighty song of power. The plane quivered and bucked for an instant, and then charged straight out across the dawn light-shadowed field. Machine guns and rifles were now cracking and banging away on all sides, and countless metallic wasps of death were hissing past the plane as it rocketed forward.

An instant later he heard the Messerschmitt's rear guns rattling away, and Freddy's wild shouts and bellows as he sprayed the Germans swarming across the field. Dave grinned, tight-lipped, eased back on the stick and lifted the One-Ten clear of the ground and upward toward the dawn sky.

"R.A.F. coming up!" he shouted, and jerked his head around for a second.

Freddy was still drilling away with his swivel gun in the rear cockpit and yelling at the top of his voice. Dave turned front, leveled off the climb and banked around toward the west and the English Channel. His heart sang a wild song of joy as the swift Messerschmitt One-Ten ripped along through the air. Victory was in sight, now. Death and danger had been defeated. In half an hour they would be over the English Channel. Another forty minutes or so and they would be well over English soil.. Back to England! Back to England with complete information about the coming Nazi drive. Names, dates, places—everything that the Nazis planned. The number of troops to be used, the list of ports where invasion barges now waited to be sent out toward England under the cover of darkness. Everything! The whole works! And now the British could—

Dave didn't finish the thought. At that moment Freddy's fist banged down on his shoulder, and the English youth's voice shouted excitedly in his ear.

"To the right and up, Dave!" Freddy yelled. "Take a look! A swarm of Nazi planes trying to cut us off. The beggars back there must have radioed to units already in the air, telling them about us swiping a plane. Get everything you can out of this blasted bus!"

"And you get back to your guns!" Dave shouted, as he found the flock of some twenty-five or thirty dots high up to his left. "We're going to have trouble! Those birds have the altitude, and they can get the speed to cut in front of us by diving. Get set, Freddy! The final lap!"

Even as the last left Dave's lips, he saw the group of dots wheel toward the east and then go slanting downward. Impulsively he jammed his free hand against the already wide open throttles, as though he might be able to get additional revolutions of the thundering Daimler-Benz engines. And although he didn't have more than three thousand feet under his wings, he slanted his own nose down slightly to gain what extra speed he could.

His prophecy came true, however, regardless of his frantic efforts to skip away and out-fly that cluster of Nazi planes. Their diving speed was plenty for them to outstrip the One-Ten in the mad race for the Channel. And when Dave and Freddy roared out from the shore, the dots had changed into deadly Messerschmitt single seater One-Nine fighter planes. And they were now charging in at breakneck speed, their guns chattering out a mad song of hate and destruction.

Body braced, Dave kept the One-Ten tearing straight at the leading German plane, and pressed the gun button on the top of his joy stick. The four 7.9-mm. machine guns mounted in the nose of the One-Ten spat flame and sound. The plane rushing in seemed to crash up against an invisible brick wall. It went cartwheeling crazily off to the side, and then curved over and down into the Channel.

"Good lad!" came Freddy's voice faintly above the roar of the engines.

A split second later Freddy emphasized his words with the chatter of his rear gun. Out of the corner of his eye Dave saw a One-Nine swerve crazily and crash straight into another German ship before its pilot could pull out of the way. The two ships fell downward, leaving behind a long column of smoke and flame. Dave shouted words of praise, sliced past yet another One-Nine charging in and then hauled back on the stick. The One-Ten power zoomed wildly toward the sky.

The maneuver, however, was not so successful as Dave had hoped. There were more Messerschmitts up there, and they opened up with a withering fire. He kicked rudder and almost went into a complete "black-out" as the terrific turning force seemed to roll his eyeballs back into his brain. He straightened out slightly, slammed down in a quick dive and caught a One-Nine cold in his sights. He pressed the gun button on the stick, and German machine gun bullets put another German out of the war.

For every German those two boys dropped out of the sky, however, three more seemed to come streaking out of nowhere. They were all around the One-Ten, underneath it and above. Time ceased for Dave Dawson. Time stood still. He became a part of the plane he flew—a sort of mechanical pilot who had no time to think or consider the next move. Every touch of the stick or rudder was both instinctive and automatic. There was smoke and flame and hissing bullets all about him. White pain ripped into his side, but he hardly felt it. His One-Ten shook and shivered as burst after burst ripped into it. His heart was cold and his brain was frozen with the realization that it could not go on forever. The One-Ten was being constantly raked from prop to tail.

Then, suddenly, it happened!

A long burst crashed into his port engine. It coughed and sputtered and then passed out completely. Smoke belched out for an instant but there were no licking tongues of flame. It was the end, nevertheless. With only one engine Dave couldn't possibly hope to get away from the swarm of Messerschmitt One-Nines wheeling and darting about them. And in that horrible moment of realization he realized also that neither he nor Freddy wore parachutes.

He jerked his head around to yell at Freddy
to hang on tight, but the words never left his
lips. Rather, a cry of wild alarm came out instead. Freddy was slumped forward over his
swivel gun. His eyes were closed, and there was
blood trickling down from an ugly bullet crease
along the left temple.

Dave took one quick glance, then jerked his
head forward and shoved hard on the stick. The
nose dropped, and the single engine started to
haul the plane downward in a terrific dive. It
took every ounce of Dave's strength on the left
rudder to compensate for the useless port engine.
With only one engine going, the plane fought
savagely to veer off to the right and into a spin.
But Dave somehow held it steady and went
rocketing down through the swarm of One-
Nines before their pilots realized what was hap-
pening.

And then, as he suddenly cast his gaze downward and to the north, his heart almost burst
with joy. Cleaving the water southward was a
British destroyer. Black smoke lay back over her
aft deck, indicating her speed. And Dave could
tell from the countless tongues of flame leaping
up from her decks that her anti-aircraft "Pom-

Pom" guns were blasting away at the sky full of German planes.

"Hold on, Freddy!" Dave got out through clenched teeth. "Don't die on me, pal. Everything's going to be jake. They haven't licked us by a darn sight. There's a destroyer down there, Freddy, a British destroyer. I'll crash in her path and make her pick us up. Hang onto everything, Freddy, old pal!"

Twenty seconds later Dave flopped the crippled One-Ten down into the waters of the English Channel. The jar flung him hard against the instrument panel, and for a brief moment all the stars in the heavens swirled and spun around in his brain. The instant his vision cleared, he stood up on the seat and waved both arms wildly at the destroyer rushing toward him. The Messerschmitt One-Nines tried to drop down and machine gun him murderously, but the destroyer's Pom-Poms kept them at a respectful altitude.

The destroyer swerved slightly and cut her speed down. In a few moments she had worked up close to the floating plane. Sailors on the low decks threw Dave a line. He caught hold of it somehow and made the end fast to the cowling brace. As the Pom-Poms continued to bark, the sailors pulled the plane close. Dave motioned one of them to jump down, and scrambled back to Freddy. Tears of joyful relief burned Dave's eyes when he found out that Freddy was still breathing. Two sailors took charge and hoisted Freddy aboard. White pain stabbed Dave's side as he scrambled aboard in turn, and he would have toppled over backwards if a sailor had not caught his arm.

"Easy does it, Fritz!" the sailor said.

"Fritz, nothing!" Dave gasped as the pain in his side started leaping up into his chest. "R.A.F. Where's your commander? I've got to see the commander at once! Get me the commander at once!"

A white blur appeared in front of Dave, and a voice said:

"I'm the commander of this craft! What's this all about?"

Dave clenched his teeth, staggered over to the two sailors who held Freddy, and took the plan paper from out of Freddy's pocket. He reeled back across the deck and grabbed hold of the railing for support. There was a thunderous roaring in his head, and red hot knives were cutting his body to pieces. He raised haze-filmed

WINGS OF THE R.A.F. 249

eyes to the destroyer commander's face, and held out the folded sheet of dirty paper.

"Think I'm about to pass out, so listen plenty close!" he said with a tremendous effort. "We're Pilot Officers Dawson and Farmer, R.A.F. Just escaped from Antwerp. Put into the nearest port. Radio Colonel Fraser to meet you. Reach Colonel Fraser at once. These are Nazi invasion plans. The—the whole works! Put—into nearest —port. Radio—Colonel Fraser—Chief—British Intelligence. Important—"

Dave knew that he was falling down into a great big black hole, but he was too far gone to do anything about it.

When he next opened his eyes, he was in a hospital bed and all wrapped around by three or four miles of bandages. At the foot of the bed stood Air Vice-Marshal Saunders, Colonel Fraser, and a major in medical uniform. He stared at their smiling faces for a moment, then turned and looked at the next bed. Freddy Farmer had at least one mile of bandage wrapped about his head, but he was sitting up and grinning from ear to ear.

"Going to sleep out the rest of the war, Dave?" he asked with a happy chuckle. "Man, is it good to see you come around! How do you feel?"

"I don't know, yet," Dave heard himself say. Then a little light seemed to flash on in his head, and memory came racing back. He turned and looked at Colonel Fraser. "The invasion attempt!" he gasped. "The plans Pierre Deschaud gave us! What—"

The Intelligence chief stopped him with a gesture of his hand and stepped around to the side of the bed.

"Everything's fine, my boy," he said in a soothing voice. "You just relax, and take it easy. You stopped a couple of bullets, you know. Take it easy and get your strength back."

"But the invasion attempt?" Dave insisted.

"Thanks to you two, there wasn't any," Colonel Fraser said with a smile. "We beat them to it and blasted the tar out of their invasion bases. Too bad you couldn't have seen it. Your pals shot down one hundred and eighty-five planes on the fifteenth. That was two days ago, by the way. It was a new R.A.F. record for a single day's bag of Goering's chaps. And that night the bombers made a mess of the invasion attempt, but before it was even attempted. So you see, there really wasn't any invasion attempt."

"But Hitler has jolly well been taught a thing or two," Air Vice-Marshal Saunders spoke up. "And it'll be a while before he thinks about trying it a second time. As the Colonel said : Thanks to you two lads, we beat them to it, and gave them a very bad trimming into the bargain, too. And it will help you to get back to active duty sooner, let me say that there'll be a decoration for you two for the wonderful job you've done."

Dave looked at Freddy, and as their eyes met an understanding passed between them. The smile on Freddy's lips faded, and he shook his head.

"You tell them why not, Dave," Freddy said.

"Eh?" Air Vice-Marshal Saunders grunted. "What's that?"

"We'd rather not be given decorations, sir," Dave said quietly. "The man who should get it, and really deserves it, is not here. He's Pierre Deschaud. He was the man who did the tough job, and—well, Freddy and I were just sort of messenger boys, you might say. Right, Freddy?"

"Absolutely!" Freddy said. "Satisfaction that we helped pull off the job is decoration enough for us."

Air Vice-Marshal Saunders looked at Colonel Fraser and smiled.

"I ask you," he murmured, "what chance has old Adolf got when he's up against chaps like these two?"

The End